# SECRET ADMIRER PACT

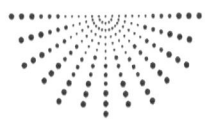

## BERNADETTE MARIE

5 PRINCE PUBLISHING
5PRINCEBOOKS.COM

Cover Art: Marianne Nowicki

ISBN Digital: 9781631123603

ISBN Print: 9781631123610

01102024-011520204

*To Stan,*
*Remember when we were just friends? Remember?*
*Ya, that was a sham!*
*I love you, forever and a day, my Best Friend!*

# ACKNOWLEDGMENTS

As always, I want to acknowledge my family who have always let the fictional characters that live in my head take my time. Thank you for embracing my storytelling and letting me spend time with them. I love you all 300 (Ya, we know it's 3000, but they get it!)

Amazing books don't just happen. There is a skilled team behind every one of them, and I'm grateful for that team. Cate finds my many flaws and persuades me to fix them for the better (and she's got a good eye for that.) Jessica finds the many missing elements that are created when you alter a manuscript as many times as you do during editing. Marianne creates the cover art that makes people pick up my books. And Laurie and Christian bring my characters to life with their talented voices. Without this team, I'd again be only a girl with a laptop making stuff up for my own enjoyment.

My readers are the heart of my storytelling. Without your love and support, there would be no reason to share my stories. Thank you for falling in love over and over again with me. I promise to continue to write as long as you show up to read. This is my world, and I love sharing it with you.

## ALSO BY BERNADETTE MARIE

# SECRET ADMIRER PACT

# 1
# MONIQUE

Outside, fireworks explode around the city, car horns blare, and neighbors are standing on their balconies cheering at the arrival of the new year.

I, on the other hand, have my head rested on my arm on the tabletop, the empty bottle of champagne still wrapped in my other hand.

I lift my head when Will rests his hand over mine on the bottle. He, too, looks as miserable as I feel.

"Happy New Year, sweetheart," he says, his words slurred from champagne.

"Sure," I say, letting my eyes close. "Can't even imagine anything happy about it."

"Cynical," he teases, but I don't have the energy to argue with him.

Lifting my head, I sit back in my chair and scan a look over him. Will's hair looks like he just rolled out of bed, but that wasn't how he looked when he'd brought me home. Alcohol and stress have had him raking his fingers through it until now it stands on end.

Will is a handsome guy, though lacking in any fashion sense.

He's my ride or die friend, has been since middle school, and I adore him.

"Are you going home?" I ask, noticing his eyes blink slower, or maybe my eyes are blinking slowly.

"No. Since you begged me to drink away the old year with you, you're going to have to let me sleep on your couch."

I was hoping he'd say that. I don't want him to leave. Tonight, I want the company.

"Do you think she's home?" I ask.

Will leans his elbow onto the table, resting his head in his palm, and he watches me. I move to mimic him, placing my elbow on the table and my head in my hand.

"She's home," he says. "I'm just afraid that maybe she's not alone."

I reach for his other hand and lace our fingers together.

"You know your living situation makes no sense, right?" I say.

"I know that more than anyone," he admits.

"I mean, who lives with their ex?"

His thumb brushes my knuckles intimately. "We weren't exes when we moved in together."

"But when you broke up—"

"When we broke up, neither of us could afford to move, remember?" he interrupts.

He always says that, but I sometimes wonder if it's true, or if he just thinks they'll get back together if they still live in the same house.

"Is she seeing someone?" I ask.

He shrugs. "She doesn't talk to me, but there have been a few nights where she didn't come home."

I shake my head. "You deserve so much more."

"So do you, sweetheart," he says.

"Valentine's Day is going to suck," I spit out the words.

Will snorts out a laugh. "That's like six weeks away."

"Yeah, but nothing good is happening in my life. No man, which means no date."

"I'll always be your date, Mon."

I give him a raspberry. He's always my date, because he's the best man walking the planet—and so out of my league—and so in love with someone else.

"I think I need to get some sleep. Are you good with having me on your couch?" he asks.

"Of course," I say, just watching him until he grins at me.

"Shall I get the bedding from your closet, or would you rather do that for me?" he teases when I haven't moved.

I don't like people in my spaces. Closets, cabinets, the refrigerator are private places. Who goes into someone's house and just goes through those things?

Well, my grandmother, and I think that's why I get so testy about it.

I don't exactly mind Will going through those places, but he knows it makes me nervous, so he never does.

"I'll get them," I say.

I just need a moment to collect myself. The past year has been a shit show, and for some reason, I keep thinking, if I just stay up on New Year's, I'll have some magic fairy fly through the window and grant me a better new year.

Not really. I'm not that kind of person. I guess I should look at it differently. If I go to bed, it closes out last year and I will wake up with a new sense of . . . I don't know. All I still feel is dread, and that's silly.

I have a great job. My condo is perfect, and I totally scored new shoes on sale at Neiman Marcus.

But I'm lonely.

My only intimate moments are with Will—but they're only in friendship.

I let go of Will's hand and press mine to the top of the table. Lifting myself from my chair, I feel heavy and unsteady.

3

Holding myself at the table for another moment, I get my bearings.

Will stands too, and when we're both steady, he reaches for me and pulls me to him.

I wrap my arms around his neck and look up at him. He's grinning at me, and I know it's because I'm drunk.

"Happy New Year, Mon," he says.

"Happy New Year," I say, but he doesn't let me go.

"I think you need a New Year's kiss."

I wrinkle my nose. "Wouldn't that be nice?"

"I think it would." He wraps his arms around me tighter. "I'd like to kiss you for the new year."

I purse my lips. "You want to kiss me?"

"Wouldn't you like to kiss me?"

"We don't kiss like that."

"I didn't mean it had to be like that—whatever *that* is. I just meant a kiss to welcome the new year."

Considering I'm anxious to send the old year out, I can't imagine a better way to ring in the new one.

"Okay. You can kiss me," I say.

"That's the most romantic thing you've ever said to me," he teases.

"This isn't a romantic kiss."

"Then why kiss? Is this why you're single?" he asks.

"You're single too. Do you remember that?" I have to get my dig in. I sometimes wonder if he does remember that.

"I think the moment is over." His arms loosen around me.

"On three," I say, keeping myself in place until he tightens his grip on me.

"Again, so romantic."

"Not romantic. Sweet."

"Fine," he agrees.

"One. Two. Three," I say as I close my eyes and wait.

When I've decided that maybe he's actually not going to kiss me, I begin to open my eyes. But that's when Will moves in.

We've spent years kissing one another's cheeks, or very quick pecks on the lips. But we've never kissed.

His lips press to mine. I close my eyes again and accept the warmth the soft kiss brings to me.

My lips are pliant under his, and they part, as do his. One of his hands moves up my back and to the nape of my neck, and it causes me to cup the nape of his neck too.

My body sinks into him a bit more, and there is a hum, or a moan, that escapes one of us.

Will is my dearest friend. There isn't anyone I'd rather ring in the new year with.

He eases back only slightly so that our foreheads rest against one another's.

I open my eyes and study him. Was I expecting more than that?

"Happy New Year," he says in a shaky whisper.

"Sure. Happy New Year."

I move from him, unsteady, and walk to the hall closet. I pull down the sheet, two pillows, and the blanket I keep for guests—that I keep for Will.

When I turn with them in my arms, he's standing right there watching me. I hand them to him and close the closet.

"Thanks," he says.

"I'm glad you're staying."

"Do you have plans tomorrow—I mean, today," he chuckles.

I shake my head and lean against the closet door because holding myself upright just isn't working for me. Only now I'm not sure if it's the champagne or the kiss.

"When we wake up, no matter the time, I want to take you to eat and celebrate your new year."

Blinking is becoming a chore.

"My new year?" I ask.

"New promotion. New outlook. New promise," he says.

"What about your new year?"

Will shrugs. "I don't see much promise in my new year."

I purse my lips. I want to argue with him, but I can't even stand up much longer.

"I'd like to go out with you," I say, easing away from the wall. "Good night."

Will studies me for a moment and moves in closer. "Good night, Monique. Sleep well," he says as he presses another soft kiss to my lips before easing back and walking away.

I watch him. He's easy on the eyes and gentle with the heart. It's too bad. Will Maxwell is the kind of guy women should be swooning over. Well, they do. He, on the other hand, is stuck on his ex. It's ugly really. He deserves so much more, and so do I, just as he'd said.

"Are you okay?" His voice comes from the living room, and I realize I'm still standing there watching him, leaned up against the closet door.

"Just taking a break," I tease.

"Do you want me to carry you to bed?"

I consider that for a moment. My body warms throughout to think he would do just that. Will is a prince. Brandy, his ex, is so stupid. She never deserved him. He's much too wonderful a man to be treated the way she's treated him.

"Monique?"

"I'm going. I'm going," I say as I turn to go back down the hall.

"I love you," he says, as he always does.

"Yeah, yeah. I love you, too."

## 2
## WILL

I figure I've been trained since birth to wait on a woman. I grew up with two moms and three sisters. I've been waiting on women my whole life.

Now, I'm sitting on Monique's couch. The sheet and blanket I slept with are folded neatly, and the pillow is stacked on top of them next to me. Now I wait for her.

I am probably the only man in the entire world who has seen her without makeup, her hair pulled up, or messed up in any way. Monique likes to make a statement with her style, and she does. She's beautiful, feminine, and not afraid to flaunt it. But even without being made up, she's equally as beautiful and feminine, in my opinion.

And that's what best friends are for—to be privy to both sides.

But in Monique's case, she will take the time to be put together, no matter how long someone is waiting for her.

I stand when I hear her bedroom door open. And, just as expected, Monique walks toward me as if she's walking in a fashion show. When she reaches the living room, she even does a little spin.

"I'm ready," she says as she lifts her white framed sunglasses to her face and pushes them on.

Her dark hair is a bit unruly by nature, but somehow, she manages it so that it flows at her shoulders in perfect ringlets and curls. My mother Anna is so envious of Monique's curls that she's threatened to cut them off while Monique sleeps. She wouldn't do it, but I'm not sure I've convinced Monique of that.

She has on a pair of distressed jeans, a tank top under a long flannel shirt, and open-toed heels, even though there's snow on the ground and it's thirty degrees outside.

On her arm is an enormous purse which I know only has her small credit card wallet, a lipstick, and a folded brush inside. That's all. My grandmother's purse is that big, and I can guarantee that there is an entire household in her purse. You need first aid? My grandmother has you covered. A snack, no worries. Gum, paper to write on, the receipt from the Christmas present she bought me when I was ten, it's in there.

I smile at her as she models for me. "You look amazing."

"That's what I'm going for," she says, walking toward the kitchen, opening a cupboard, and taking down a jeweled Starbucks cup. "I'm ready."

"A coat?" Sometimes I'm the only reasoning she has.

Monique makes it a point to look out the window. The sun shines three hundred days a year in Colorado. Heatwave or snow, it's sunny. Monique takes that as a sign that she doesn't need a coat.

"I'm good," she says, and what it really means is that I'll be freezing when I give her my coat later.

I can't help but chuckle and follow her out the door.

---

The restaurant we decide on is in Golden. There is a short line on New Year's Day, and Monique shivers next to me as we stand on the sidewalk.

I don't suppose it helps that she made me stop at Starbucks first so she could have some iced drink put into that fancy cup she carries around.

"Would you like my coat?" I ask.

"I'm fine," she says, just as she had when we were at her house. But she moves closer to me, so I wrap my arm around her.

We only wait ten minutes, and when we are seated, Monique sits across from me. Her legs are crossed, and she pulls the flannel shirt closed as if it'll warm her.

"Have you been here?" she asks me.

I nod as I study the menu.

"Did you bring Brandy here?" she asks.

I lift my eyes to look at her. "I was with Brandy for five years. I took her a lot of places."

Monique purses her full pink lips. "She's over you," she says.

"It seems that way," I agree, lifting my menu back up.

For the moment we are silent, until the server comes to take our orders. I order a coffee, and grin when Monique orders a mimosa.

My head still hurts from the champagne we consumed last night. I'm not sure how she can possibly stomach more, except that it's bougie, and Monique is all about bougie.

As the server walks away from our table, Monique settles into the booth, still pulling her flannel close around her.

"You need to date," she says.

"I'll date when I'm ready."

"When will that be? You've been broken up for the past six months. And still living together."

I chuckle. "We just live within the same dwelling. Do you know I haven't actually seen her in three months?"

"You're sure she's still living there?"

"I'm sure," I say, picking up my water and taking a sip.

I know Brandy is still living there because I can smell her perfume. Her jacket hangs on the back of the kitchen chair. Her coffee mug sits in the sink every night.

I sip my water again, because it chokes me up thinking about it.

Monique is watching me. We've been friends for so long, I can tell she's scheming, and she knows I'm wallowing in self-pity.

"What?" I ask.

She taps her chin with a perfectly manicured finger. "Nothing."

"You're lying. I know you too well."

She licks her glossed lips and grins. "You want her back?"

"I do."

"I don't know why. But I want you happy," she says. "I have an idea."

"Are you going to let me in on it?"

She considers for a moment, but before she can speak, our drinks arrive. She picks up her mimosa and toasts me with it.

"I'll make her notice you," she says. "But I'm not going to let you in on it quite yet."

"She doesn't like you. You can't just show up and tell her you think she should take me back."

"I would never. Let's be clear, I still think you should move out and move on. But if my best friend wants the woman of his dreams back, I want him to have that. And I promise you the woman of your dreams by Valentine's Day."

"And you can make this happen?"

"Do you trust me?" she asks as she lifts her glass to her lips.

I've never trusted anyone more, but she's scheming. I can't even imagine what she has in mind.

"I trust you."

She smiles, and it lights into her eyes.

I've just become a puppet in Monique's latest game. I'm not sure that it'll end the way she's thinking it will, but I trust her. And what do I have to lose? If I want Brandy back, I need to do something to get her to notice me again.

# 3
## WILL

I chuckle when I open the refrigerator to pull out a yogurt for my morning commute. Shaking my head, I close the door. All of the yogurts I bought last week are gone.

One of the interesting parts about having a roommate that no longer speaks to me, or shows her face when I'm home, is that she still eats the food I buy, and when I make coffee, she drinks it.

Admittedly, I don't mind. Monique is convinced that it means Brandy is using me. I think it's comforting, as if she remembers that I'm still here.

I pull my travel mug from the cupboard and fill it with coffee. Once I secure the lid, I reach for my coat and pull it on. Sticking my hand into the pocket to pull out my keys, I feel something else.

From my pocket, I retrieve a paper napkin with writing on it. *Will-*

> I've been watching you. I think you're very handsome. I'd love to get to know you.
> Love,

*Your Secret Admirer*

The note has me laughing. It's written in Monique's hand-writing, and I can't even imagine why she—

I look back down at the napkin and grin.

So, this is Monique's wise idea to get Brandy to notice me? I now have a secret admirer?

Am I supposed to leave these little notes around the house?

I can hear Brandy moving around her room. I look at the note again and consider it.

Instead of taking my coffee mug with me, I set it on the note. She'll notice that I forgot my coffee, and maybe she'll see the writing on the napkin.

Well, I have nothing to lose with Monique's little game.

Grabbing my messenger bag, I hike it up onto my shoulder and head out to work.

---

As is the norm, my phone rings as I'm leaving my office and heading to lunch.

"So now you're my secret admirer?" I ask as I answer the phone, knowing Monique is on the other end.

Her laugh filters through and brings me a bit of warmth as I step outside in the cold.

"Why, Will, I have no idea what you're talking about," she says with another laugh. "I take it you found a note?"

"I did."

"And what did you do with it?"

"What was I supposed to do with it?" I ask as I step to the corner with the small crowd that waits for the traffic light to change so we can cross the street.

"Seriously? You didn't just throw it away, did you?"

The light changes and the crowd moves across the street. "Oh, honey, it was so cute, I would never throw it away."

"Then what did you do?"

I can't help but laugh as I walk toward the deli where I placed my lunch order. "I left it on the counter under my travel coffee mug."

"Under your coffee mug? She'll never see it there."

"Sure she will. I always take that coffee mug. It looks like I forgot my coffee. And I left the napkin exposed."

Monique sighs on the other end of the phone. "You'll tell me if she says anything?"

"Of course I will. Am I supposed to expect more notes in my pocket?"

"A secret admirer never writes just one note," she says with some confidence. "Let me know if anything happens with that note. I have more plans."

"Oh, you do?"

"If you want Brandy back, then that's what I want for you."

There's a hitch in her voice. She would rather I move on and find someone new. I, on the other hand, like familiarity.

No matter what happens, I can guarantee that Monique will always be on my side.

"So, we have a little shakeup in the office this morning," she says, changing the subject. I can hear the bracelets on her arm clink together, which means she's talking with her hands, as she does.

"Do tell," I say as I open the door to the deli and step inside.

"We have a new CEO."

"Just like that? No announcement?" I ask as I walk toward the shelf where they put out the preorders.

"They fired Neil. Rumor has it he was making some unsanctioned deals."

I pick up my bag and head back out of the deli. "So, how is the new guy?"

"Will, he's hella sexy," she whispers into the phone.

"You can't date the CEO."

"Says who?" she asks with a giggle, which I haven't heard her do in a long time, which means she's in full flirt mode.

"That spells disaster," I tell her.

"It spells adventure."

"Having an affair with the boss is an adventure?" I tease.

"Of course. There's the no-no factor, for one. What if you get caught? What if you both get fired? Sometimes it's the adventure."

I walk toward the fountain that sits in the courtyard of my office building, and I sit down on the side of it. The water is off for the winter, but the statues in the center still make it an impressive piece of art.

"Don't you want security? Don't you want forever?" I ask as I open the bag from the deli.

"Do *you* have security and forever?" she asks.

I'm not answering that. "I just think you deserve someone who will take care of you. And I don't mean that you need to be taken care of," I add quickly, because I know this woman, and it'll come back at me. "I'm just saying, it's nice to be in love and part of something."

"Right," she draws out the word to make her point. "Is that why you live with your ex? Because it's something special? It's love? It's forever?"

"Mon—"

"No, do tell. I mean, I'm all in for a relationship like that."

I let out a long breath. "So you're going to hit on your boss?" I change the subject back to her.

"I'm going to flaunt it all," she laughs. "He's that sexy."

"And if you land him, then you, too, will have a date for Valentine's Day?"

"Most certainly."

"Best of luck to you," I say.

"You could help," she says.

"You want me to help you hit on your boss?"

"I'm helping you," she says.

I wince. "What do you want me to do?"

"I don't know. Let's make a pact. I'll be your secret admirer, and you can be mine."

I laugh. "You think that's going to work?"

"You tell me when you get home. If she's talking to you, it worked."

"It sounds childish, Mon."

"It sounds like a plan, Will. Dinner Thursday?" She changes the subject, again, and knows I'll say yes, because we always have dinner together on Thursday.

"Wouldn't miss it for the world."

"Good. I have it under good authority your secret admirer will have something for you."

# 4
## MONIQUE

I couldn't wait to hear about Brandy's reaction to the note. Actually, I'd be okay if she tore it up and stirred it into his coffee. I can't stand the woman, and she can't stand me. Oh, she tolerates me. There really isn't any choice there. Will and I have been best friends since the seventh grade. I don't believe that all soulmates have to be romantically involved. And I think Will and I are just that—soulmates.

I'm not going anywhere and Brandy has always known that.

But, if Brandy is what Will wants, well, then I grudgingly want the same for him.

Sitting at my desk, legs crossed, I bounce my Givenchy heel on and off my foot as I consider our next move. I haven't done the secret admirer bit since college, but it's never failed.

I need to slip him another note. I can't just hand it to him. There always needs to be an element of surprise; this way his reaction is genuine, just in case she's there when he finds it.

It has me wondering what he'll do as my secret admirer to get my boss to notice me.

First, I need coffee.

I push back from my desk and pick up my coffee cup. The

coffee in it is cold, so I head out of my office to refill it. As I turn the corner to the break room, I wave at Val, who catches my attention, and then I crash into a hard body.

Coffee splashes up and out of my cup. It's cold against my chest as it soaks through my blouse. But there are drops of hot coffee too, and I notice as my new boss jumps back. He's holding his coffee mug out to the side, but wincing because his hand is covered in hot liquid.

"Oh my god!" I shout as our bodies separate.

My blouse is soaked. His tie and shirt are wet as well, and there's coffee on his suit jacket.

"I'm so sorry," he says as he turns back into the break room. He sets his coffee on the counter, turns on the cold water at the sink, and runs his hand under it.

"Are you hurt?" I ask, following him.

"Stings a little. I'm okay," he says, turning off the water and examining his hand.

I set down my mug and reach for the roll of paper towel at the same time he does. Our hands actually slap together, and we each jump back.

I'm not sure which one of us laughed first, but from there, it just became more funny.

Here we are, two strangers in the break room, both covered in coffee, and we're laughing. I see Sue from HR walk into the room and retreat just as quickly when she sees us.

My new boss holds out his hand to me. "Jay Cresswell, the new CEO," he says.

I stick out my hand and shake his. We laugh harder because both of our hands are wet.

"Monique Trafford," I say through laughter. "Bookkeeping."

He gives me a little nod as he puckers his lips. "Well, Ms. Trafford, we won't forget one another, will we?"

"Can't imagine we will," I say, looking down at how my blouse is clinging to me and leaving not much to the imagination.

I reach around him for the paper towel and begin to blot my blouse, though it's not going to help.

I have a sweater on the back of my office chair. You know the kind that you leave there for the summer days when the air conditioning is turned up so high and you're freezing inside? It'll really make a statement with my Givenchy shoes and pencil skirt.

With the paper towel still pressed against me, I look up at my boss, who is watching me.

He has deep blue eyes, and hair that begs to have my fingers tangled in it. I know just how hard his body is because it crashed into me.

"I should get back to my desk. Maybe I can hide out in my office today," I tease, and he chuckles.

"I am so sorry," he says again, as if this was all his fault.

"I'm sorry this is how I got to meet the new boss," I giggle, and toss my hair over my shoulder as if I'm at a bar and flirting with some random. It causes me to stiffen a bit when his lips twitch as he smiles at me. "I'll see you around," I say as I turn to walk out of the break room.

---

Me: *OMG! OMG! OMG!*

Will: *Do I dare ask what you're up to?*

Me: *I just met my boss*

Will: *I assumed you met him when you told me how hella sexy he was*

Me: *Can I call you?*

Will: *You have never asked before*

I wrinkle my nose at that and then press the call button.

"Seriously, Mon, what's up?" he answers.

"We ran into each other in the break room," I whisper, even though I'm in the confines of my office.

"Great place to meet new people," he says.

"No, I mean we really *ran into* each other. We spilled coffee all over each other."

He laughs. "Sexiest meet cute I've ever heard of."

"It wasn't cute," I argue. "My blouse is ruined, and he burned himself."

"So you marred your boss?"

"It wasn't all my fault."

Will is still laughing. "Why are you calling me?"

I look out the door to the people walking through the office carrying on in their normal ways. Turning my chair toward the window, I look out at my view of the other buildings that surround ours.

"Will, he's all that," I say.

"You can't date your boss."

"You don't understand," I argue.

"No, you don't understand, Mon. It never ends well."

That doesn't even matter to me in this moment. It's been a bit since I've dated anyone, and I'm over casual. What if Jay Cresswell is the man of my dreams? What if he can offer me everything I've ever wanted?

Not that I know what I really want.

I've never been one to be tied down. I like playing the field. I like the conquest.

Casual is okay with me, but to actually be admired and loved, that's what I want deep down.

I want what Will gives to Brandy, even if the sentiment is never returned to him.

"Mon, I have to go. Are you good?" Will asks and I realize I've taken a journey into my own head.

"I'm fine."

"I'll see you Thursday, and I love you."

"Yeah, I love you too."

# 5
# MONIQUE

It's cold enough to warrant me wearing a coat. Luckily, I found a long beige peacoat in the back of my closet. It's long enough to touch the top of my boots, keeping my knees mostly warm, and it's fashionable, so I don't look as if I'm hiding under it. Though the puffer jackets that everyone else in Colorado owns are practical, I don't see me ever owning one. REI and Patagonia are not part of my retail therapy routine.

Taking a few moments in front of my mirror, I examine how I look. I don't know why I won't wear a coat in the winter. This one is classy.

Looking at my phone, I check the time. Will should just be arriving at the bar. He won't expect me for another fifteen minutes, because that's my way—leave them waiting and make an entrance.

I walk through the door of the sports bar where Will and I meet each week for dinner. He always arrives before I do and takes one of the high-top tables with the best view of the big screen TVs around the bar.

"You do realize that every man in this place watches you when you walk through here?" Will says as he stands and moves to kiss me on the cheek.

"Are they gawking or admiring?" I ask in his ear.

Will eases back. "There is a fine line," he says, his eyes locked on mine. "But it makes me look good."

"And what does that mean?"

"It means that you walk in that door every week and right to me. I'm a god among mortals here."

That makes me laugh.

He's not like all the guys in the bar. Will has had me in his life since we were twelve, and though he often looks me over, I never feel as if I'm being judged. He simply appreciates me—for me.

"Nice to see you wore a coat," he says.

I shrug out of my coat, and Will takes it from me, folds it and lays it over the back of one of the empty chairs.

"It went with the outfit," I say, drawing his attention to me.

"As long as it's fashionable and not just practical," he teases as he pulls out my chair.

He waits until I take my seat before he sits back down.

Waving down the server, he asks me what I want to drink.

"I'm feeling like a glass of wine," I say.

"Really? After the other night?"

I grin at him and then wink. "That was champagne. Besides, wine doesn't affect me like it does you."

He orders me a red wine and then orders our usual appetizer platter, which we count as a dinner.

Crossing my legs, I lean my elbow on the table, my Pandora bracelet slipping down my arm.

"What did Brandy say about the note?" I ask, because in the past two days, he hasn't mentioned it. It leads me to assume she never saw it, or just doesn't care.

Will purses his lips and leans in on his forearms, wrapping his hands around his beer.

"I haven't seen her or talked to her, but she noticed the note."

I raise a brow. "You know this for sure?"

He nods slowly. "I'd set the coffee cup right on top of the note. It had even left a little coffee ring on the napkin." He grins. "The cup's placement didn't match up to the ring."

"That's how you know she read it?"

Will shrugs. "It's something, right?"

I tap my finger to my lips. "It's a good thing I'm ready with another note."

Shaking his head, he reaches for my hand and gives it a squeeze. "This seems a bit childish," he says.

"She read the note. I think it's intriguing."

"Intriguing," he says, laughing as he eases back in his seat as the server delivers my wine. "What's the end goal?"

"To get her to talk to you."

"She's likely to still tell me to go to hell."

I lift my wine to my lips and take a sip. "But she'll have to talk to you to tell you that."

When the appetizer platter arrives, I set my napkin in my lap and dive in, taking the first cheese stick from the top of the pile. Usually, I watch what I eat. But on Thursdays, I'm all in for the fried delights and wine. And then, every Friday I pound the water just to get the excess fried carbs out of my system.

Will picks up a fried pickle and blows on it. "What about you and your boss?"

"Old news. I already shagged him," I deadpan, and Will's eyes go wide.

I can't help but laugh as I bite into my cheese stick and pull it back, leaving a rope of cheese between my teeth and my fingers.

Will sets down his pickle and wipes his fingers on his napkin.

"Seriously, Mon," he scolds.

"I'm kidding," I say around the mouthful of cheese. "You're too gullible."

He shakes his head at me and pops the pickle into his mouth.

I chew my cheese stick, sitting back in my chair. Dabbing the napkin to my lips, I think about what he's asked.

"Nothing has happened with the boss," I say. "I can't decide if he's avoiding me because he saw right through my blouse that day, or if I just don't turn his head."

"Maybe he's busy being the boss," Will suggests.

I shrug. "I guess that could be it. Or maybe he's not interested."

"It is possible, you know. You might be the most beautiful woman in a room, but maybe he's not into beautiful."

That has me laughing. Will is easy with the compliments.

I pick up my wine and sip. "I just need to get his attention."

"I think you need to move on," he says.

I raise a brow. "I need to move on?"

"You shouldn't be trying to get your boss' attention. It'll never end well."

"And maybe you should move on too," I say with a bite. "Because remember, in your case, it already ended."

He takes another sip of his beer. He knows I'm right, and yet, I'm still going to slip him another note, signed by his secret admirer.

## 6
## WILL

The light over the kitchen sink is on, and I hear the faint click of a door closing as I walk into the apartment. It's not unfamiliar. It usually means that Brandy heard me coming in, and she hurried out of the room.

Living together after we broke up had to be one of the worst ideas ever. I can't let go, and she can't afford to move.

Tomorrow I work from home, which I do every Friday. Brandy tends to get up earlier than normal so that she's not around when I come out of my room. It's become our norm. It's irritating as hell.

I step into the kitchen and open the refrigerator to put my takeout container inside. After having dinner with Monique every Thursday, where we indulge in fried bar food, I always order a sandwich for lunch the next day. It's my treat, since I don't go into the office.

I set the box on the shelf and head to my room.

———

I wait until I hear Brandy leave in the morning before I exit the confines of my bedroom. On the days I work from home, I take full advantage. I have on a baseball cap, a T-shirt, and a comfy pair of sweats. There is never a Zoom meeting scheduled, and if I have to talk to a client on the phone, well, they never see the stains on my shirt.

Opening the refrigerator, I pull out the orange juice. I've been making a point to drink my fair share since Brandy and I broke up. I used to buy it for her because she loves to have a glass in the morning. When it became something I bought out of habit only, and she was still drinking it, I decided I'd better drink it too. There are a few moments every day where my stomach hurts like crazy, because of the orange juice, but, it's the principle.

As I twist off the top to the juice and take a long, satisfying swig, I look at the box I'd put into the refrigerator last night. On top of it is a note on a crunched up napkin.

> *I've been thinking about you and those beautiful eyes.*
> *XOXO*
> *Love, Your Secret Admirer*

There is a set of lip prints on the napkin, in the same shade that Monique has worn since high school.

I laugh at the note written in her handwriting.

I twist the cap back on the juice bottle, set it on the shelf, and look at the note again.

Picking it up, I examine it. It has juice from the tomato on the corner.

Closing the refrigerator door, I walk back to my room. Instead of texting, I call Monique.

"Did you leave me another note?" I ask as she answers.

"Yes."

"When?"

I can hear a door close and I assume she's closed her office door so she can talk to me in private.

"Last night," she says.

"Where?"

"I left it with you at the restaurant."

"No," I shake my head even though she can't see me. "Where did you leave it?"

"In your to-go container. Did it fade on your sandwich?" she asks with some concern.

"I don't know if it faded on my sandwich or not. When I found it, it was on top of the box."

"I put it inside the box," she confirms.

"I get that," I say, grinning down at the note. "Brandy must have opened the box and seen the note."

Monique lets out a tiny gasp followed by a giggle. "That's even more perfect than I thought."

"And she set it out so I'd know she saw it."

"See, you're getting to her."

"I think I am," I agree, setting the napkin on my nightstand. "Thanks, love. I owe you one."

"You owe me a million."

---

Monique turned down my dinner invitation, opting instead to go out for drinks with the girls from work. Sometimes I forget that she's not just there for me.

Now I'm standing in the kitchen with the refrigerator open. I scan the bare shelves for something I can put together for dinner for myself.

I stiffen when I hear the key in the door, and it pushes open.

With the refrigerator door still open, I watch as Brandy walks into the apartment.

Even though I live with the woman, I realize how long it's been since I've seen her.

She stops when she sees me, and we just look at each other.

Her blonde hair is pulled back, and she's in a pair of jeans and V-neck t-shirt. Fridays at her office are casual, but she can pull off jeans and a T-shirt and still look professional and put together.

"Hey," she says almost so softly I barely hear it.

"Hey," I say in return, still standing with the refrigerator open.

"Worked from home today?"

"Yeah," I say, knowing she knows that.

"I won't bother you," she says as she walks toward her room.

"Do you have dinner plans?" I finally manage a full sentence.

She stops as she walks back through the apartment. "No. Not tonight."

"Me either," I say, finally shutting the refrigerator door. "I could order a pizza. Would you be interested in sharing?"

She's gripping her purse in front of her as if she's nervous. When did we get to this, where we couldn't even have a conversation with one another?

"Are you sure?" she asks.

"Yeah. All meat?"

The slightest smile curled up the corner of her mouth. "That sounds great." She reaches inside her purse and pulls out a twenty. Sliding it across the breakfast bar, she leaves it there. "My contribution."

"I'll buy."

"No," she says quickly. "I eat enough of your food. I'll chip in."

Oh, so she notices she eats all the food I bring in? I don't say anything to that. If I didn't like it, I would stop buying it. When she eats what I put in the refrigerator, I take it as a sign that she still knows I'm there.

"I'll get it ordered," I say.

"I'm going to go change. Let me know when it gets here."

I nod as she walks to her room and closes the door.

Picking up my phone, I order the pizza. Then I text Monique.

Me: *We're having pizza together*

Monique: *You're welcome*

I shake my head. I don't know what more I expected. She's not going to be truly happy for me, but she won't deny me this, either.

7

# WILL

Brandy walks out of her bedroom the moment I close the door on the pizza delivery guy.

She sits down on the counter stool and watches me as I carry the pizza to the counter and set it down. Without a word, I turn and take down two plates from the cupboard and set them in front of her.

As if it were normal, this silent little dance we're doing, Brandy dishes out the slices, and I take down two glasses and fill them with wine.

Carrying the glasses around the counter, I set the glasses in front of the plates and sit down next to her.

She keeps her head down and begins to pick the meats off of her slice and pop them into her mouth. It's something she does when she's deep in thought.

I'm not sure where to start a conversation. It's been months since we've been in one another's presence this long.

I bite into my slice as she lifts her wine to her lips and sips.

"How was your sandwich?" she asks.

I lower my slice and realize I never set out napkins. I stand, walk around the counter, and take the roll of paper towels off of the holder.

I tear off a piece for her, and one for me, which I wipe my mouth on.

"It was good. Doesn't change much from week to week," I say, walking back to my seat.

Brandy continues to pick the meat from her pizza. "I saw the note that was in the box," she finally says, without looking up.

"Yeah, I didn't know that was in there until I saw it in the fridge."

She lifts her eyes to me for the first time. "You didn't know?"

"No."

Now she picks up her slice and takes a bite. "I saw the other note too," she admits.

I only nod. What am I supposed to say to that? I mean, I left it for her to find.

I sip my wine and watch as she sets her pizza down and wipes her mouth.

"Do you know who it is?" she asks.

I do everything in my power to keep my face neutral. "No. I don't."

She nods slowly. "Well, it must make you feel good. I mean, it's nice to have someone notice you."

"You're right. It does feel good."

Brandy picks up her wine and sips. "Did you do something fun for New Year's? You didn't come home."

This is interesting. She noticed that? Was *she* home all night? I realize I don't even know.

"Yeah. I had a good time. You?" I ask.

"Oh. Yeah. I had a great time." She sips her wine again. "I appreciate you ordering the pizza. I figured I was just going to have some cereal and head to bed."

"I was just going to veg on the couch and catch up on some shows, so it wasn't a big deal."

She takes another bite of her pizza. "What were you going to watch?"

"There are so many Star Wars series now, I was going to dive in and binge. I've gotten behind."

Her lips turn up into a smile. "You still like Star Wars?"

"Well, you never stop liking Star Wars," I say factually.

Brandy nods. "Would you mind if I watched with you?"

I figure it was a darn good thing I hadn't taken a bite of my pizza. I just might have choked.

Is this attention just because of a few secret admirer notes? I guess Monique knew what she was doing. Now I owe her.

"I'd love to have you join me. We could start now."

Brandy picks up her plate and her glass of wine and moves to the couch.

I guess we're staying in tonight—together.


Two and a half episodes into the Mandalorian, and I know she's not interested anymore. She stopped asking questions and is now scrolling on her phone. But, the silver lining, she hasn't up and left yet.

When my phone chimes on the counter, we both look up. I stand and retrieve my phone.

For the first time ever, I'm not excited to see Monique's text. I must have let out a grunt of displeasure too, because it prompted Brandy to ask, "What's wrong? Who is it?"

No matter what I say, it ends our evening. Not that our evening was going anywhere, but we were at least speaking.

If I tell her it's Monique, that'll get a reaction.

If I tell her I have to go pick up a friend who's been drinking, that'll get a reaction.

Neither of which is going to be a positive reaction.

Maybe if the secret admirer notes have been working because

she's jealous, perhaps telling her that Monique needs me right now would help, too.

I bite down on my lip as I consider my next move.

"It's Monique," I say, and Brandy's lips grow tight. I don't think she even knows she did anything of the sort. "She needs a ride."

"Now?"

"Yeah. She went out with the girls after work, and she needs a ride home."

"She's drunk?" Brandy asks, and she's obviously appalled.

"She's had a few drinks and doesn't trust the girl who was designated to drive."

"Can't she Uber?"

Oh, this has gotten under Brandy's skin, and it's taking everything inside of me not to laugh.

"She's not a fan of Ubers. I'll go get her. There's more pizza and wine," I say, as if it'll remind her we had a nice evening together.

"The pizza is cold. Besides, you drank. Should you be going to get her?"

"I had one glass of wine two hours ago. I'm good." I turn toward the door and take my coat off the hook. I slip it on and fish the keys from my pocket. "I'll see you tomorrow," I say and watch her eyes grow wide and then narrow.

"Whatever," she says, standing from the couch and walking to her room. Without another word, she shuts the door and locks it.

I chuckle to myself as I leave the apartment. Monique is going to have a guest on her couch tonight, I decide. If a text got that kind of reaction, wait till I walk in tomorrow morning with a bag of Brandy's favorite bagels, after spending the night out—with Monique.

8

# MONIQUE

I'm still holding the last drink I was handed. As nice as it was for the group of guys at the bar to buy us all drinks, I don't drink anything I didn't watch the bartender pour.

"Mon, we're going to go to the bar down the street," Val says, her words slurring a bit.

"I have a ride coming. I'll be fine," I say.

The guy that handed me the drink slides up next to me. "I'd give you a ride," he says, but I have to be honest, I'm not sure he means a ride home in his car.

"All good. My boyfriend is only a few minutes away," I say right before I see Will walk through the door.

I wave and Will walks toward me.

I set the drink on the nearest table and envelop him the moment he gets close. Then, because I know the drink guy is watching, I kiss Will.

It's no peck that I give him. No. I sway against him, causing him to wrap his arms around me as if to hold me up. Then I slide my mouth over his and kiss him.

I'll admit, I'm surprised that his lips go pliant under mine as they do, and then open.

My arms are draped around his neck, and his hands are low on my back. When his tongue sweeps against mine, I go light-headed. I didn't even drink the drink I'd had in my hand, but this kiss has made me drunk, and I sure hadn't expected that.

When I ease back, I bite down on my lips as if to hold the kiss there a moment longer. He grins and winks at me. Okay, he knows what I was doing, but why did it shake me up so much? And why did he take that kiss so far?

I turn back to Val and the drink guy. "Do you want a ride too, Val?"

She shakes her head. "I'm going with the girls. Dawn will drive us home."

"Are you sure she's okay?"

"Oh, yeah. She never drinks," she slurs.

I don't hang out with these girls often enough to vouch for that. I wave, and hand in hand, Will and I walk out of the bar.

The moment we step outside, Will takes his coat off and wraps it around me.

"I know you own a coat," he teases before taking my hand again and lacing our fingers together.

"I left it at work, actually."

"I'm impressed. You wore one to work."

"Hey, I'm sorry about that back there," I say, and Will stops walking.

"Why?"

"The kiss. I just—"

"You were just making a point. I get it. No foul."

Wow. I guess the earth moving for me was just my knees giving because of the alcohol, though I haven't had that much to drink.

When we reach his car, which he parked two blocks away, he opens the door for me and I slide inside. He must have had the seat heater on when he drove to pick me up because it's still slightly warm.

Will hurries around the car and climbs in the other side.

Rubbing his hands together, he blows into them before starting the car.

"Have you eaten?" he asks because he knows I don't have food at my place.

"We ate before we went to the bar," I say.

He nods. "We'll drive through and get some hamburgers. You'll want something in your stomach."

I watch him as he pulls from the curb. He's happy. I haven't seen him happy like this in a long time.

It's not that Will is unhappy, and especially around me, but when he's happy for other reasons, it resonates through him.

"I'm sorry I interrupted your evening," I say.

"Honey, you could never interrupt my evening."

"So you had pizza and that was it?" I ask.

He's grinning. "Actually, we had pizza and wine, then watched TV together. It was an epic night."

I sink into my seat. "I really did mess stuff up for you."

He reaches for my hand and holds it in his. "Nah. She was feeling me out," he says. "She mentioned the note you left in my box from dinner last night. I told her I didn't know who had been leaving me the notes."

"So you think she's just curious?"

He shrugs. "Sure. But it got us talking. Then you texted—"

"And I'll bet she told you to not come get me."

"She didn't, exactly. She thought you should get an Uber. But even if she did say it in just the way you're suggesting, I would have come to get you no matter what. You know that."

I do know that. That's why I called.

He turns at the stoplight and heads toward my condo. "It got under her skin a bit," he says. "Now she's curious as to who's into me. I'm not about to tell her no one is. And I'm staying at your house tonight, just so you know."

"Will, I'm fine. You don't have to—"

"I know," he interrupts. "I'm staying so she's driven crazy all night wondering where I am."

I let out a little laugh. "And that's supposed to work to get her back?"

"Sure. I mean, just two secret admirer notes worked to get her to talk to me. Maybe the mystery of me not coming home will do wonders."

I'm not sure about that logic. I mean, a little jealousy over secret admirer notes is one thing. Thinking he's doing things that he's not, that's completely different.

I'm conflicted, because I still want him to have what he wants. But I don't want to lose my best friend.

"So the guy at the bar wasn't the boss?" he asks as he turns into my parking garage and I wonder if he realizes we didn't stop for hamburgers.

"No. That was just some guy who bought me a drink and then followed me all night wanting me to drink it."

"That sounds sketchy."

"Hence the reason the drink was still full in my hand when you picked me up."

"I don't know why I'd ever worry about you. You have a good head on your shoulders."

Sure. If I did, I'd date someone like him instead of going to bars with people from work—and I'd never forget my coat.

# 9
## MONIQUE

Will slept on my couch and was gone before I got up Saturday morning. I didn't talk to him all Sunday either.

Maybe his plan worked. Maybe he got home from a full night out and Brandy was there waiting for him, ready to scoop him up and take him back.

I guess he doesn't know I've had a restless weekend. He doesn't know because he hasn't called me or texted me, which is odd.

He doesn't know that I'm exhausted sitting at my desk because for two nights I've lost sleep thinking about that kiss we shared.

Okay, it wasn't a shared kiss, as in we both went in for it to get something out of it. I was using him to get that guy to back off. I kissed him. I hadn't expected him to react the way he did. I guess I wasn't expecting myself to react the way I did either.

But, honestly, it became something more.

We'd kissed on New Year's, and that had been something we'd never done like that before. But now, this kiss at the bar…

I blow out a breath, pick up my coffee, and sip.

William Maxwell has never turned my head. Don't get me wrong, he's a looker. But we've been friends since zits and braces. He knows every guy I've dated. I know every girl he ever pined after.

It wasn't the first time I've ever used him for the *I have a boyfriend* bit either. But still . . . we've never kissed like that.

We've slept in the same bed and never had anything happen, because we're not into one another. We're friends. And that's why that innocent kiss—well, these TWO kisses, now—are messing with my head.

"Monique," Val says my name, and I look up from my computer screen to see her standing in the doorway of my office. She's holding an enormous vase of roses. "These just came for you," she says.

"For me?" I stand as she walks into my office.

"Yes. They smell so nice." She sets them on my desk. "Who'd you meet when we went out the other night? Someone with some money, huh?"

"No one who would know to send me flowers," I admit.

"C'mon, open the card. I'm dying here," she says, nodding her head toward the card buried inside the flowers.

My head is racing, and I can't for the life of me figure out who they could be from.

I pick up the card and tear it from its tiny envelope.

*There is no beauty in the world that compares to yours. Enjoy.*
*Love,*
*Your Secret Admirer*

My eyes go wide and so do Val's. Only her mouth turns up into an enormous grin and mine gapes open.

"A secret admirer? Dang, Monique. This arrangement has to

be over a hundred dollars. Someone must really like you to send you this."

"I don't understand," I say.

"Enjoy the attention, honey. Someday you'll get married, and he won't care about you within six months," she says, holding up her left hand to flash her wedding ring. "Trust me."

Val turns to walk out of the office, stopping only long enough to acknowledge Jay Cresswell standing in my doorway looking in.

"Those are pretty," he says, and my throat begins to close.

The man hasn't talked to me since we dumped coffee on one another after he started. Now he's standing in the doorway to my office, grinning at my situation?

"Thank you," I say, tucking the card back into the arrangement.

"Boyfriend?" he asks, walking into my office.

"No. I mean . . . no. I don't have a boyfriend."

He nods slowly. "Parent? Is it your birthday?"

I shake my head. "No. My birthday is in July," I say, though I don't know why I offered up that information.

His eyes light up and he grins as he touches the petals of one of the roses.

"Whoever they're from, they must really think a lot of you."

"They're just from a guy I know," I say. "I'm just a bit surprised by them."

Since we made a pact to pass each other secret admirer notes, I assume the bouquet is from Will. And if it is, I guess it worked. It got Jay Cresswell to talk to me. Though it's much too expensive for Will to be sending me gifts. That wasn't the deal.

"I'm not surprised," he says, lifting his eyes to meet mine. "You're an attractive woman. It doesn't hurt that you're friendly and smart, too."

I'm sure the expression on my face is one of absolute confusion. How does he know I'm friendly and smart? Seriously, the man met me one time in an awkward situation.

"Thank you," I say, and my voice shakes a bit.

Jay smiles and turns toward the door before turning back. "I'm ordering in sushi for lunch. Boardroom at noon?"

Is that an invitation to have sushi? Or is that an invitation to eat my lunch in the boardroom while he eats his sushi?

What does it matter? He's giving me his attention, and that's what I wanted, right?

"I'll be there," I say.

Jay gives me a little nod, still smiling at me.

I look at the arrangement that sits on my desk. The scent is making my head swim. Will can't afford to be buying me flower arrangements that cost this much. The secret admirer ploy is one thing, but I scrawled notes on napkins. This . . . this is asinine. When we made this pact, this wasn't what I was thinking.

I sit down in my chair, pick up my cell phone, and text Will.

Me: *Thank you for the flowers*

I take a picture of them and send it to him.

Will: *Those are nice. Who are they from?*

Me: *Don't play games. I know you sent these*

I pick up the card again. It's not written in Will's handwriting. Then again, this is the kind of order that would have been called in or ordered online. I'm surprised the card is handwritten at all.

Will: *I didn't send them. But they're nice*

I can feel the blood drain from my head.

Me: *You didn't send these?*

Will: *No, Mon. Hey, gotta go. Love ya!*

Me: *Sure, love you too*

I send my reply and set down my phone. If Will didn't send these, then who is playing my game against me?

## 10

## MONIQUE

At noon, I walk into the boardroom with my lunch tote in hand. Still unsure if I'm joining my boss for lunch, or just sitting there with him.

The boardroom has twelve chairs. Six of those chairs are taken with heads of other departments. There are three trays of sushi on the table as well as bottles of water on the credenza and a tray of brownies.

This isn't quite what I'd expected, but at least I understand the invitation now.

Val waves me over to sit next to her. "Did you figure out who the flowers were from?" she asks.

"No. They didn't come from the guy I'd thought."

Dave whistles low. "I saw the bouquet. Someone is grateful for you."

I don't like how he says it like that, but I don't have time to argue because Jay Cresswell walks into the room and everyone hushes.

"Thank you all for joining me. I hope I got rolls that everyone would like. If you're not into sushi, I hope you'll have a brownie," he says as he laughs and takes his chair. "I just wanted to get to know you all."

To say I'm disappointed in this being a "getting to know you" meeting is an understatement. The way my boss had lingered in my office, I was sure this was supposed to be an intimate lunch.

Val hands me a small paper plate with a few pieces of California roll and shrimp tempura roll on it. She knows I'll only eat vegetable rolls or cooked ones.

For the next half hour, Jay Cresswell tells us about himself, his plans for the company going forward, and has us introduce ourselves.

But right as we make it all the way around the table, and we finally get to my introduction, which is last, he dismisses us and thanks us for our time. I'm the head of the bookkeeping department and I'm not important enough to be introduced?

I wrap my brownie, which had been passed around before we were dismissed, in a napkin and drop it into my lunch tote as I stand.

"Monique, hold back a moment," Jay says, looking up from a conversation he's having with Doug from purchasing.

I nod and stand there until Doug leaves the room, closing the door behind him.

"I'm sorry we didn't get to your introduction," Jay says, walking around the table toward me.

"No problem. Thanks for not keeping us all day," I say, as if I have a lot of work I'd rather get back to.

"Have a seat," he says, motioning to the chair next to me.

I sit and cross my legs. He sits down next to me, turning so his knees face mine.

"So, tell me about you," he says, easing back in his chair.

"Me?"

"Yeah, introduce yourself. Just as everyone else did."

I look around the room that was only moments ago filled with people doing just this. So why am I here alone?

Touching my bracelet, I consider what I'm going to say. But I finally realize that he's made it so that we're alone.

Wasn't this what I told Will I wanted?

Lifting my head, I make eye contact with him, again touching my bracelet because it's intimate. I know how to flirt. I do it all the time. Now is not the time to wig out over who I'm alone with.

"Well, you know my name," I say with a hint of playfulness.

"I do," he replies with what I consider a hint of playfulness too.

"Head of bookkeeping. I've been with the company now for going on two years. Graduated from CU Boulder, go Buffs," I add, and Jay winces. "Not a fan?" I ask.

"CSU," he rattles off the rival university. "Go Rams."

I let out a low hum and raise a brow. "This just isn't going to be a friendly work environment, is it?"

"Oh, I don't know. Just tell me you're not a Raiders fan, and we can probably move forward," he teases.

"Who are the Raiders?" I say deadpan, and he studies me for a moment before he realizes I'm kidding.

"That's more like it." Jay smiles and I notice that when he does, it crinkles up the sides of his eyes. Will's eyes do that too when he smiles wide. It's comforting. "Native to Colorado?" he asks.

"Born and raised. You?" I ask, and then shake my head, realizing that the flirting is taking over the actual conversation with my boss.

But he's smiling. "Upstate New York, then a very short stint in Iowa, before coming here in the sixth grade."

"Transplant," I say firmly. "At least you're not from Texas or California. I think it's safe to say we can be friends."

*Friends?* What the heck?

Jay eases back in his chair. "Alright, friend." He's smiling at me. "I shouldn't keep you much longer." He sits straighter. "Thanks for staying and chatting."

This is my cue to go. I turn to gather my plate with the intent of throwing it away.

"I'll get all of that," Jay says.

"Are you sure?" I ask, and he nods. "Thank you for lunch," I say as I stand, and so does he, only we're so close together that we smack foreheads.

Jumping back, my hand immediately goes to my head. "I'm so sorry," I say, wincing at the sharp pain between my brows.

"You? I'm sorry," he says, rubbing at the same spot on his head. "We seem destined to hurt one another," he laughs as he says that, but suddenly a bolt of seriousness goes through me. I want the man's attention, and I seem to have it. But what if we both get hurt? What if we hurt one another and we work together?

Jay reaches out and touches my arm.

"Are you okay? You just went pale. Did I hit you harder than I think I did?"

I blink and look up into those fantastic blue eyes that are filled with concern.

"No," I say, a bit too breathy. "I'm fine. I'm fine," I repeat. "I should get back to work."

"Thanks again for spending your lunch in here."

"My pleasure," I say, gathering my notepad and the lunch bag I'd carried in. "I'll talk to you later."

My face is hot from the blood that has risen to my cheeks, and I swear I can feel a knot forming on my forehead as I hurry toward the door.

I pull on the door with a bit too much force and it flies back much harder than I think it should and knocks me right in the forehead, right where Jay and I have already collided.

My notepad and lunch fall to the floor, and I'm seeing spots. I gasp for breath, but things are getting a bit fuzzy.

I hear my name, but then that's it. My vision goes dark.

# 11

# WILL

There is a bump on Monique's forehead that is raised right between her brows. By tomorrow, she might have two black eyes too.

"When you want to impress someone, you go all out, don't you?" I ask, sitting in the chair in front of her desk.

"I didn't call you to come get me so you could sit there and tease me," she says, lowering the bag of ice she's been pressing to her face.

"Are you sure? I thought that was protocol."

She shakes her head and winces. "I look like an idiot."

"You look like someone pushed open a door and hit you in the face."

"Well, it sounds better than I remember it. I thought I did this to myself," Monique says, adjusting the ice and putting it back on her nose. "I thought I clocked myself."

"If it's any consolation, Val feels really bad about knocking you out."

Monique finally smiles, taking the ice off her face again. "She's going to be making up for that one for a long time," she threatens. "Especially if I end up with two black eyes."

"Can I take you home now?" I ask. "I mean, I can't be seen in public with you looking like this. It'll ruin my image."

Monique dismisses my diss with a shake of her head. "Thank you for coming to get me."

"I love you. I would never leave you to look like that alone," I tease again.

"Careful, Mr. Maxwell, or I'll tell people you did this to me."

"No one would ever believe you. I'm much too kind a person to inflict harm on anyone."

She puckers her lips. "You need a woman who understands that."

"Don't I have one?"

She raises a brow. "Do you mean Brandy? Because no. I don't think she knows that."

"Well, I have you," I say, and I notice a flash of something in her eyes before she narrows them at me.

"You'll always have me, but you deserve better at home," she says, standing, gaining her balance, and then picking up her purse from the top of her desk. "Will you feed me?"

I laugh. "Are we going in public or ordering in?"

"Do I look like I'm ready for public display?"

I walk around the desk and take the bag she carries all of her extra items in, and then I lean in and kiss her on the cheek. "You always look ready for public display, no matter what."

"Yep," she sighs. "You're too good for her. You're too good for anyone."

---

It's nearly ten o'clock when I walk into my apartment after staying with Monique after work. She's going to have two black eyes in the morning and said she wasn't going into the office, but she's too much of a team player not to.

47

As soon as I open the door, I hear the TV, and then hear it click off.

I have to assume that Brandy was waiting up.

I close and lock the door. I hang up my coat and messenger bag, and when I turn, she's standing near her bedroom door.

Having lived together for months without seeing her, I don't know if I'm startled by her presence or genuinely thrilled that she hadn't run out of the room completely.

"You're home late," she says softly.

I take a moment to take in the sight of her. She has her blonde hair pulled up into a messy bun on top of her head with tendrils that have escaped framing her face, and she's wearing her flannel pajamas. The woman is always cold.

"Yeah. I didn't mean to interrupt your TV watching," I say, surprised that she was watching TV in our shared space, and not adding anything of value to her question in the way of an answer.

"Oh, I was done," she says as she yawns, but she doesn't go into her room. "Were you working late?"

She's still fishing. "No. Just helping out a friend."

Brandy's lips twist to the side before she asks, "With your secret admirer?"

And how do I play that one off? Yes, my secret admirer, I humor myself.

"Monique. She got hit in the face and needed a ride."

Her eyes go wide, and I swear that she's holding back a smile. I'm going to assume that I'm not seeing it correctly, though. Surely she'd be concerned.

"Is she okay?" she asks.

"She'll be fine. She'll probably have two black eyes in the morning."

Now her face appears to show some shock. "Did she wreck her car? Did a man do that to her?"

I keep my expression as blank as I possibly can. Her concern humors me. "Val, in her office, walked through a door just as

Monique was getting ready to open it. It was an accident, and Monique was the victim."

Brandy's mouth twitches until she does smile. "Oh. Well, I hope she's okay."

"She'll be fine. She has an enormous pair of black Chanel sunglasses that she could wear for the next week."

A small chuckle escapes from Brandy as she sets her hand on the knob of her bedroom door. "Tell her I hope she heals soon."

Interesting.

"I will."

She lingers there for another moment before opening her door. "Goodnight," she says.

"Goodnight."

I wait until she disappears into her room and then I scrub my hands over my face. I cannot believe that Monique's little secret admirer game has Brandy talking to me.

Pulling my phone from my pocket, I walk to my bedroom and shut the door.

Me: *OMG she was waiting up for me!*

Monique: *That's nice*

Okay, so she's not as excited by the prospect as I am. I get that. Still, I owe her for this moment.

Me: *How's your face?*

Monique: *Still better than yours*

Harsh, but I'll take it.

Monique: *I'm just kidding. You're nice to look at.*

That has me grinning down at my phone. My mom Sheila always said that Monique and I would have the most beautiful kids together. My mom Anna would then comment that maybe with my eyes and Monique's everything else, our kids would be models at birth.

We always laughed that off. My mothers are romantics, even though they've always known that Monique and I are more like brother and sister.

As I sit down on my bed, I rethink that. No, we are definitely just best friends, and not sibling-esque at all. If we were, that kiss she planted on me the other night wouldn't have affected me as much as it had. I understood the need for it. I just hadn't expected to lean into it, to take it deeper, to feel it.

I press my hand to my stomach and close my eyes. I'm actually kinda dizzy just thinking about it.

Her mouth was warm and soft on mine, and when she opened up to me, I couldn't help but taste her, and she reciprocated.

I blow out a breath. Maybe we need to make sure that never happens again. I mean, I'm all for being the assumed boyfriend when she needs an out. I've done it before. But kissing her, that seems to have only confused my body.

No, the only woman I want to be kissing is Brandy, and maybe that'll happen in the near future.

I look back down at my phone.

Me: *Sweet dreams. I love you*

Monique: *Yeah, I love you, too*

## 1 2

# MONIQUE

I do, in fact, have two black eyes. More like it, I have a bruise on the bridge of my nose, but yeah, I look like I was in a back-alley boxing match and lost.

The bruising is so unfortunate that I can't even wear my sunglasses all day to hide it. Instead, I've holed up in my office with the lights low and the door closed. We've been working on reports and budgets for Jay as he gets familiar with his CEO role, so there was no calling out. As the head of the department, I'm expected to be here.

I keep to myself until lunchtime, and since I brought my own lunch, I stay in my office. With my cup of yogurt, a half of a turkey sandwich, and a bag of carrot sticks, I fuel myself for the rest of the day.

When my phone chimes, I smile down at it when I see Will's name pop up.

Will: *How are you feeling this morning?*

Me: *I feel just fine. I look like crap*

Will sends me a smiling face emoji with sunglasses and a question mark.

Me: *Too sore to wear sunglasses. I'm locking myself in my office today*

Will: *I have a coffee delivery coming your way. Make sure you let them in*

About the time I start to reply, there is a tapping at my office door. I wince, but that only hurts.

The door opens slowly and Jay peeks his head around the door. "Can I come in?"

I figure he was there when I passed out. I might as well let him see the damage.

"Sure."

He steps into my office, closing the door behind him. In his hand he has a frozen coffee.

"This just arrived for you. I told them that I would deliver it."

"It arrived for me?" I ask as Jay walks toward my desk. "Who brought it?"

"Uber driver," he says as he nears my desk. "Do you have something I can set it on? It's got condensation on it."

I nod, open one of the drawers on my desk, and pull out a stack of napkins. I lay them on the top of my desk and Jay sets the drink down before taking a seat on the edge of my desk. The closeness and intimate gesture has me inching my chair away, only slightly.

"How do you feel?" he asks.

"I feel fine. I look horrible."

"I wouldn't say that." Jay moves his hand to my chin and lifts my head to examine my face. "You're still beautiful."

My mouth goes dry, and I lick my lips to moisten them.

Jay lingers, with his fingers still on my chin, and smiles before he lowers his hand. "You didn't order this coffee, did you?"

I look at the cup he'd set on my desk. The double chocolate, frozen coffee with whip from the coffee shop down the street melts into the napkin Jay had set the cup on. That's when I notice the writing on the cup.

*Monique—Enjoy! Love, Your Secret Admirer*

I blink hard and read it again.

Swallowing, I shake my head and lift my head to look up at Jay. "No."

"Your secret admirer strikes again?"

The roses that were sent to me yesterday are on the credenza behind me, in front of the window. And now the coffee.

I know the coffee is from Will. He told me he'd sent it up. He didn't tell me he was going to make it from my secret admirer. But he said he didn't send the flowers.

I press my fingers to my forehead because my head is spinning, but that only makes me flinch when I hit the bruise.

Jay is still sitting on the corner of my desk, and now he's grinning.

"I guess so," I say in response to his question.

"Same guy?"

I shrug. "I don't know who it is," I say, because I don't know who sent me the flowers.

"Well, you seem to be quite popular. I'm glad I get to spend time with you at work. It appears the competition on the outside is fierce."

I shake my head. "I don't know about that."

"Do you have that budget report?" he asks, and abruptly I realize that he's still my boss, no matter how intimate these past few moments have been.

"I was just finalizing it," I say. "I should have it ready by this afternoon."

He nods and stands. "I assume you're staying out of sight?"

I snort out a laugh. "For the next few days, yes."

"Why don't we plan on meeting in here at three this afternoon. You can walk me through the report, and you won't have to be seen outside your office."

He's dreamy in every way.

"That would be fine," I say, but my voice shakes a bit.

Jay moves to the other side of my desk. "I see you're taken care of for lunch?"

"I am."

"Then I'll see you at three." He moves to the door, looks back one more time, then steps out, closing the door behind him.

I look at the coffee on my desk and pick up my phone.

Me: *I got my coffee. Thank you. My boss carried it in*

Will: *That's good, right?*

Me: *He knows about the flowers yesterday too*

Will: *Those aren't from me*

I still can't even imagine who they are from if they aren't from him.

Me: *I come across like some slut!*

Will: *You appear to be admired*

He sends a string of heart emojis.

I sit back in my chair and look at the coffee and the flowers. Admired.

Adjusting my bracelet on my wrist, I text Will back.

Me: *Thank you*

Will: *Get back to work. I love you*

Me: *Yeah, I love you, too*

## 13
# WILL

Monique: *There is a cup of coffee on my desk, again. Secret admirer, again?*

I look at my phone as I walk into my office building. I have on gloves, so I can't even reply, and I'm so freaking cold, I'm not going to reply right away.

She then sends a picture of a regular cup of coffee.

Well, whoever her other secret admirer is, they don't know her too well. She'd brew herself a cup of coffee, but she would never—never—drink one from a paper cup from a coffee shop.

I step into the elevator and pull off one of my gloves with my teeth, keeping it clenched there.

Me: *I know better than to send you that. You didn't really think that was from me, did you?*

Monique: *You sent me coffee yesterday*

Me: *I sent you dessert in liquid form. That's just coffee*

My phone rings in my hand and I answer it, even though I'm surrounded by others in the elevator.

"Don't mess with me," Monique begins to argue. "I was trying to help you out. I got Brandy to talk to you with some notes, like we agreed, but this . . ."

"Sweetheart, I only sent the one frozen coffee. This cup of coffee and the flowers—not me."

She lets out a breath, and it's shaky. "This freaks me out."

"Well, then I'm glad I know who my secret admirer is. I feel safe."

The woman next to me grins up at me, and I smile back as the elevator lands on my floor.

When the doors open, I step out and walk down the hall to my office.

"Mon, enjoy this. If nothing else, you have your boss's attention."

"Sure. He thinks I have men pining for me and that I'm a klutz. I'm hiding in my office with two black eyes."

"And I know for a fact you're just as beautiful as always."

"Jerk," she says.

I drop my messenger bag on my chair behind my desk.

"Dinner tomorrow?" I ask.

"I'm not going in public like this," she says. "No. I'm not going to dinner."

"Fine. I'm dropping by after work to check on you."

"You're talking to me. There's no need to check up on me," she argues.

"I want to."

My coworker stops by my desk and points to his wrist.

"Hey, I have a meeting. I have to go. I'll see you tonight."

"Fine."

"I love you."

"Yeah, I love you too," she says.

---

The state of Monique's refrigerator—it's always empty. She keeps enough in there to pack sad lunches. I'm glad she's saving money by doing so, but really, she needs more than yogurt and fruit in her life.

When she opens the door, I'm standing there with a wide grin and a bag of groceries.

But looking at her, my smile fades.

"Maybe we should have you looked at," I say.

"I told you I look hideous."

She turns back and walks into her condo, plopping down on the couch as I walk in and close the door.

"I didn't mean you look hideous. I meant it's darker." I set the bag of groceries on the coffee table and sit down next to her. "I guess bruises do get worse before they get better, don't they?"

"I don't know. I've never looked like this."

She pushes her hands up into her wild, dark curls and then falls over on the couch, resting her head on a throw pillow.

"I should just quit."

That has me laughing. "Over this? Honey, remember the haircut, first year on the job?"

She groans. "Are you kidding me with that? Of course I remember it."

"You didn't stop going to work then, and that was worse than this."

Monique swings her body back up and rests her head on my shoulder. "You're very sweet. You're a liar, but you're sweet."

"I love you. I know you're self-conscious about this, but, honey, it's not so bad."

She lifts her head and looks at me. "Thank you."

"I brought you some groceries. I'm sure your fridge is empty and you're not going to the store to shop, so . . ."

Her shoulders drop and I watch as her eyes fill with tears.

"Mon, I didn't mean to—"

She waves a hand in the air and purses her lips, trying to hold in the sob that I know wants to break free.

I pull her into me and hold her. Her tears soak through my shirt and her body quivers against me.

"What's wrong?" I ask, running my hand over her hair and down her back.

"I'm a mess of a person, and you know that."

I kiss the top of her head. "You're anything but a mess of a person."

"I am. Look at me. I'm alone. When men try to hit on me at a bar, I call my friend to hurry and pick me up. I can't even walk through doors without running into people and spilling coffee or getting knocked to the floor." As she hiccups a sob, she chuckles slightly. "Brandy's a lucky woman. Why can't I find a guy like you?"

I give her a little squeeze. If Brandy thought she was so lucky, maybe she wouldn't be my ex.

"Sweetheart, you have me," I say, and she shakes her head and eases back from me.

"You know what I mean. I know I have you. Heck, since I was twelve, you've been my rock. It's just been a long time since I've had a man who was interested in me—who loved me."

I can't even argue that. The last man Monique was involved with broke her heart into a million pieces, and that was years ago.

She falls in love easily, but doesn't stay in love easily.

She allows me into her private space, but no one else.

I lift my hands to her face and wipe away the tears from her cheeks with my thumbs, then hold her chin so that she's looking right at me.

"You're going to find that again," I promise.

"Do you really think so?"

"I know so. Any man who loves you is a lucky man."

Monique's pouty lips turn upward into a smile. "Thank you," she says, resting her hand on my chest. "Why don't you take Brandy to dinner tomorrow. Maybe things will work out with you."

"Maybe," I say, lowering my hand, but at this moment, I only want to take her to dinner. It's our tradition. "I'll let you put everything away. I know you'd rather no one be in your space."

Monique purses her lips. "You know that doesn't apply to you, right? I mean, if I can't trust you in my refrigerator, who can I trust?"

I study her bruised and beautiful face. "That means a lot."

"You mean a lot," she says before leaning in and pressing a very gentle kiss to my lips. "Now, put away my groceries and go home to your woman. She'll be waiting for you."

## 1 4

## WILL

Again, I hear the TV when I open the door to my apartment. This time, though, it's not turned off the moment the door opens.

I hang up my coat and messenger bag and step into the living room.

Brandy looks up from her position on the couch.

"Hey," she says, tucking her legs up under her.

"Hey," I say, watching her watch me. "How was your day?"

"Good. We had a stellar year, last year, and they treated us to lunch and gave us each a bonus," she says, smiling.

It's been a long time since I've seen her smile in my direction. Sure, I had nothing to do with the reason, but she's talking to me —and smiling.

"That's fantastic," I say.

There's a silence that falls between us, so I move back to my messenger bag, pull out my travel coffee mug, and head to the kitchen.

While I'm standing at the sink washing my mug, Brandy moves into view, standing against the counter, watching me.

"Did you have dinner? I mean, I know you didn't come directly home from work."

I bite down on the inside of my cheek and consider my answer. "No. I didn't have dinner," I say. If I tell her where I went, this conversation is over. I won't lie—but I'll avoid.

I rinse out my travel mug and set it in the drying rack before turning around and pulling the towel off of the oven door and drying my hands.

"I got a big salad at the deli. I only ate half. The other half is in there if you'd like it," she offers, pointing to the refrigerator.

"Thanks. I just might."

When she lifts her thumb to her mouth, I know she's run out of small talk, but she doesn't want to leave. I don't want her to leave either, so I move to the refrigerator and pull it open. She's gnawing on the side of her thumb when I turn back around with the salad in my hand.

Because I can't stand to watch her cause damage to herself, as she does when she chews on her thumb, I reach up and guide her hand down—something I used to do when she was stressed she and didn't even know what she was doing.

Brandy blinks hard and tucks her hand behind her. "I didn't even realize I was doing that," she says.

"Old habits are hard to break," I say, wondering if she understands that I mean her biting her finger, and me stopping her.

She looks out toward the TV. "If you had something you wanted to watch on TV, it's all yours."

I pull a fork from the drawer, open the salad container, and lean up against the counter. "There's nothing I was looking forward to watching. In fact, I need to do some work on a code I'm working on," I say.

She nods. "Work tends to come home with you, doesn't it?"

I shrug as I fill my fork with lettuce. Yeah, I'm going to eat this, but I'll need something more later. There's no way this is going to hold me over, but it's the principle.

"I'll leave you to eat," she says and turns to leave the kitchen.

"You don't have to go anywhere," I say. These are big steps. I want her here. "Hey, do you have dinner plans tomorrow?"

Her brows rise and she lifts her thumb to her mouth again, before dropping her hand and clasping it with the other.

"Tomorrow is Thursday," she says.

"Yep."

"You have dinner with Monique on Thursdays."

Oh, this is taking everything not to smile at that. "Usually I do."

"But not tomorrow?"

I shrug again, taking another fork full of salad. "She's a little self-conscious about going into public. Two black eyes," I say as if to remind her.

"Are you sure about going to dinner with me?"

I lift another fork full of lettuce to my mouth and study her. "Of course I'm sure."

Brandy bites down on her lip. "Okay. I think I'd like that."

I do everything in my power to keep my face neutral. "Cool. You decide where you want to go."

"Can't we go where you and Monique go each week?"

"Sure," I say, stabbing more lettuce with my fork. "But we could go anywhere."

"No. I'd like to have those nachos again. It's been a long time."

"Yeah, it has."

Brandy smiles and it lights in her eyes. "I'd better get to bed. Have a good night."

"Yeah, you too."

I watch as she walks away and disappears into her bedroom.

I can't eat any more salad, and at the same time, I'm not hungry for anything else. I dump the salad in the trash, throw the fork into the sink, and hurry to my bedroom.

Pulling my phone out of my pocket, I fall onto my bed and text Monique.

Me: *She said yes!*

Text bubbles appear, disappear, and appear again. I watch and wait for Monique to respond. Instead, my phone rings.

"Tell me that was for the dinner invitation, and you didn't ask her something more serious," Monique says the moment I connect the call.

"For dinner," I verify.

"That's good, right?" she asks.

"Of course it's good. This is what I want. She was waiting for me when I got home. She offered me her leftover salad for dinner. And when I asked if she wanted to go to dinner, she asked if we could go where you and I always go because she wants the nachos."

Monique is quiet for a moment. "It sounds like everything is going in the right direction."

"It does. How long do I wait until I make a move?"

Now Monique laughs weakly. "Why are you asking me? You have a history with this woman. Make your move when you think it's right."

"I lost this woman. Obviously I don't know what I'm doing."

She lets out a low hum. "When the timing is right, you'll know."

"Right. I guess you're right."

"I'm always right," she says.

"When are you going to make your move?" I ask.

"I want him to make the move."

"Sounds like he just might do that."

She giggles. "Maybe. We'll see."

"Do you need me to send you another secret admirer gift?" I ask as I roll to my back.

"You really didn't send the other things?"

"I really didn't send them."

"Maybe I shouldn't make any moves until I know who the other secret admirer is," she says.

"Look at you go, Mon. You have the boss that you think is so sexy giving you attention. You have a secret admirer, and you have me. You're reeling them in."

"You make me sound like a slut."

"No, I'm making you sound irresistible."

I hear her sigh. "You're too good to me."

"Yeah, well, you let me get into your refrigerator without supervision," I tease.

"Only you," she says.

"Goodnight, Mon. I love you," I say.

"Yeah, I love you too."

15

# MONIQUE

The darn bear in my chair nearly scared me to death. One hand went to my chest and the other to the light switch to see who was in my office.

I can't help but just stand there and stare at it.

It's a plush teddy bear nearly the size of an actual adult. There is a red ribbon around his neck, and a stupid grin on his face.

If Will sent this, I'm going to kill him. What am I supposed to do with this thing?

Val walks up behind me and looks over my shoulder.

"Did we get a new employee?" she teases with a slight jab with her arm into mine.

"Who put this here?" I ask, turning to look at her.

She winces at the sight of my face, which she caused, and yeah, I know she feels terrible about.

"I don't know who put it there. Someone who got here early, I guess. Maybe it was Cresswell."

My brows pinch, and that hurts, so I try to calm my expression. "Why would he do that?"

"Because you're a catch, Mon," she says as Courtney from purchasing steps up and looks over our shoulders.

"This secret admirer of yours is pretty serious, huh?" she asks.

"Who put this here?" I ask her.

She too winces at the sight of my face, but her smile quickly returns. "I didn't see anyone come in."

I purse my lips. "Where is Cresswell?"

Courtney shrugs. "All I know is he has meetings today, off site."

Then it wasn't him, no matter what Val thinks.

Seriously, if this was Will . . .

I head into my office and the two ladies go about their day.

I move the bear from my chair and plop him into the corner of my office. I'm going to need help getting him home.

With my phone, I take a picture of it and send it to Will.

Me: *This isn't funny*

A few moments later I get an emoji with the brow raised.

Will: *What is that?*

Me: *It's a stuffed bear. It was at my desk. It's the size of me. This has gone too far!*

Will: *I didn't have anything to do with that bear. I am sending you coffee, but . . .*

I throw up my hands, fall into my chair, and call him.

"You seriously didn't send me this?" I ask.

"Mon, I seriously didn't send you that. I'm sticking to cups of coffee—seriously," he adds.

My mouth has gone dry as I look out the door of my office to the people who are rolling in for the day and getting settled. No one looks my way. No one else stops by my door. Who has access to the building when we're not here?

"This is a little creepy," I say, and Will laughs.

"You remember you started this."

"So you did send it?"

He laughs again. "No, I didn't send it. This is called karma."

"Isn't karma supposed be bad stuff?"

"Does it always have to be? I mean, you're helping me. Brandy is talking to me. We have a date tonight. I sent you coffee and now someone else is pining for you too."

I have to contemplate this karma thing.

"I'm a little freaked out by it," I admit.

"Then decapitate the bear and put his head on a stick outside your office door."

I let out a groan. "I'm not going to do that."

"It would send a message."

"The bear is cute, and this is not his fault."

"There are always casualties in war, Mon."

I look at the bear, who is looking up at me with that tight smile. "The bear is cute."

"I guess it's settled. Secret Admirer strikes again. And your fancy, frozen coffee should be there in fifteen."

I can't help but smile at that. "You really are sending me coffee?"

"And a bagel. I know you probably didn't eat breakfast and you need to."

Resting my head back against my chair, I grin at his words. "You're too good to me."

"So you keep saying."

"I'm going to miss you when you and Brandy get back together."

The line goes silent for a moment. "Why would you miss me?"

"She's not going to let you have me in your life to the same extent. There's going to be a new set of rules," I explain.

"I don't like those rules. I'm not going to let that happen."

This is how he lost Brandy in the first place. He didn't abide by the rules. He kept me close, and that made her push further away.

When I look up, Val is standing in the doorway with the frozen coffee and the bag with the bagel.

"This just showed up." She raises a brow. "Secret admirer? What's going on, Mon?"

I grin up at her and then turn my attention back to Will.

"I have to go. I just got a delivery," I say, my words laced with humor.

"Oh, whoever could have sent you something so fancy?" he teases. "Have a good day, Mon. I love you."

"Yeah, I love you too."

Val walks in and sets the drink and bag on my desk. "I love you? Seriously, what's going on? You have a boyfriend," she says surely because she'd been there the night that I kissed Will at the bar. "And you keep getting secret admirer gifts? Are you playing the field?"

I snort out a laugh. "Will sent me the coffee and the bagel. He's just being silly," I say. "And he's not my boyfriend. He's my best friend and has been since I was twelve."

Val nods. "And the flowers and that bear?" she asks, pointing to the monstrosity in the corner.

"I have no idea."

"Really?"

"Really."

"Is that freaky?" she whispers.

I have to give that some consideration. Do I mind? Do I think it's freaky?

"I don't know," I admit. "It's nice that someone notices me. It's nice that they think of me. But, yeah, I guess it is a little freaky. I mean, the bear was in my office."

Val puckers her lips. "I can't believe you don't have a boyfriend, anyway. You're a catch, Mon. Even with two black eyes," she teases.

"Gosh, thanks."

"I also can't believe you aren't dating the guy at the bar. I saw that kiss, and then I saw him caring for you when he came to pick you up the day I smacked you with the door."

I grin up at her. "He's in love with someone else, and really, we're more like brother and sister," I say, but that kiss as the bar was anything but family friendly.

Val shrugs. "If you say so. He's a catch. Maybe you should make him *not* in love with the other woman. I think he's into you."

"Well, he's not. But he's a great guy."

Val bats away my comment with her hand and turns to walk away.

I look at the coffee and bagel. Brandy doesn't deserve Will. I guess I will never think anyone deserves him—including me.

## 1 6

# WILL

Brandy had called and let me know that she'd have to meet me at the bar. She'd been caught up at work.

Like any other Thursday, I sit in the bar at a high-top table, a beer between my hands.

Since I'm a regular, the other regulars give me a nod. A few of the guys give me a little grin. I wonder what their expressions will be when the sexy brunette with the curls isn't who sits down with me.

I guess I'll find out in a second because Brandy just walked through the door.

Brandy hurries toward my table. She's sensible. She has on a long, warm coat, a scarf around her neck, and gloves on her hands. Her cheeks are pink from the cold, and her walk is hurried as if she's cold.

I hop off my chair and stand as she walks toward me.

"Hi," she says with a heavy breath. "It's freezing outside."

I smile down at her as she shivers, shaking off the last bit of the chill.

"Let me take your coat, and we'll get you something warm to drink," I offer.

She nods as she begins to unwrap herself.

I hold out my hands as she gives me her gloves, scarf, and eventually her coat. Underneath, she's dressed casually, appropriately.

I tighten my smile as I think about the contrast between her and Monique.

Monique would have hurried in here in heels that have to be uncomfortable, and I'm sure dangerous on cold streets. She'd have had on a dress or a pair of slacks that flare at the bottom. Brandy has on a nice pair of jeans and a sweater.

"Thanks," she says, and I realize I'm just staring.

I take Brandy's coat and accessories and set them on the chair next to me as she climbs up on the stool.

When I take my seat, I notice those who always watch Monique walk into the bar are now looking at me curiously. I guess they noticed that she didn't arrive, and must be equally as confused by Brandy's presence. Seriously, I wonder what's going through their heads.

With her hands folded atop the table, Brandy looks around. "This place hasn't changed, has it?"

"I think that's part of its charm," I say as I wave down the server. "Do you want a glass of wine?"

She wrinkles her nose. "I think I'll have a beer. Whatever you're drinking."

I order the drink and we sit silently for a few moments. When the server returns with the beer, she asks for our order.

"What do you and Monique usually get?" Brandy asks.

"The sampler," I say. "But you get whatever you want."

"The sampler is fine," she says.

The server puts in the order on her handheld device and disappears.

"Thanks for the invite," Brandy says looking from me to the TV overhead, and back to me.

"You're welcome."

She wraps her hands around her beer. "I was nervous coming here with you."

I raise a brow. "Why would you be nervous?"

Her shoulders drop. "We're not a couple. We haven't spoken in months," she says, as if that was the reminder I needed.

"It's nice to be on good terms again," I say.

Taking a sip of her beer, she scans the room and studies the patrons. "There's a lot of guys here."

"It's a sports bar."

She nods. "I was just thinking that maybe your secret admirer is one of the wait staff."

I chuckle and then take a sip from my beer. "Is that why you wanted to come here? You want to figure out who my secret admirer is?"

"Don't you?"

I'm grinning, and I'm sure I look like the biggest idiot. "Not really."

Brandy's brows draw in. "Do you know who it is?"

*Yes*, I think. But, still, I'm not going to tell her that. "I think it's a game. I don't take it all too seriously."

"You should. Someone really likes you," she says, and there is a hitch in her voice. "Wouldn't you want to be with someone who really likes you?"

I study her as she's looking at me. I'm confused by all of this now. I want *her* to like me. The notes were for her to notice and get jealous over. To this point, it's been working. She's talking to me. We're out on a sorta-date. I don't want to seek out anyone else.

"Well?" she asks, urgent for an answer.

"Of course, but I don't think anyone *working* here is the person I want to be with."

Did I say that with enough conviction, or a gaze in her direction that lets her know how I feel about her?

Brandy folds her hands in her lap and swallows hard. "Who do you want to be with?"

I study her.

The corner of her mouth twitches as if she's nervous about what I might say.

I suppose this is an all or nothing moment. If I tell her and she accepts it, I get what I was looking for. If I tell her and it makes her angry, nothing changes.

"Honestly, I want to be with—"

My phone rings and vibrates on the table. It's Monique's ring, and Brandy knows it.

Her hopeful look darkens as her face heats and her slight smile flattens. She picks up her beer and takes a long pull.

I pick up my phone and answer curtly. "What?"

"Well, that's sassy."

"What do you need, Mon? I'm kinda busy."

Monique lets out a playful hum. "I thought you were at the bar. I didn't realize things had escalated to—"

"They haven't. Do you need something?"

Brandy's expression softens. I suppose me being so blunt with Monique has piqued her interest, even if she's only hearing one side of the conversation.

"I just wanted to know how it was going," she says.

"Fine."

"It doesn't sound fine."

"Because you're on my phone," I say a little too harshly, or that's how it sounded in my head.

"Ohhhh," she draws out the word. "I'm just hungry for cheese sticks."

I close my eyes and run my finger over the bridge of my nose. "You can DoorDash from here, you know."

"Maybe."

"Mon," I say pleading.

"Fine. I'll let you go. Don't make any sudden moves though—

you know what I mean. She's ghosted you for months after she broke up with you. I just don't want you getting hurt."

"I get it," I say, giving Brandy a weak smile.

"Take it slow."

"I got it," I say a bit firmer.

"Let me know how it goes."

"Will do."

There is a brief moment of silence before Monique says, "I love you."

I draw in a deep breath. We end every call with those words, and have since junior high. Though, I'm usually the one that initiates them. But right now, it's just not the right time. "Yeah, ditto," I say before I disconnect the call and turn off the ringer.

17

# MONIQUE

I have paced around my condo for two hours. Will is getting exactly what he wants, and I'm hiding out with two black eyes.

Had I gone tonight, Brandy wouldn't be there.

Had I gone tonight, I wouldn't be hungry.

Had I gone tonight, Will would have told me he loved me like he does every time we talk.

I plop down on my couch. This is stupid. I'm the one who got him into the position he's in—the position he wants to be in. Will wants Brandy, and now he has her back.

What I have to remember is that even when he was with Brandy, I still had him in my life. He's my best friend. He's not going to go anywhere.

I pick up my phone and scroll through my socials. Even that's boring. Dropping my phone on the couch, I stand up and walk to the kitchen. Pulling open my refrigerator, I smile down at the items Will had brought. There are packages of fresh berries, sliced veggies, meats, and cheeses. Everything I need to make a charcuterie plate is right in front of me.

I need to not worry about Will and Brandy. I'll never lose him. He will always show up to pick me up at a bar, or bring me groceries when he knows I won't go out, and he'll always tell me he loves me.

I swallow hard with that thought. He didn't actually say it today.

I'll give him a pass. Tonight is important for him, and I should have left him alone.

Pulling the items from the refrigerator, I set them on the counter and begin to make myself a plate. I'll talk to Will tomorrow. I owe him an apology and a huge thank you for taking care of me, even when he's not around.

---

When my alarm goes off, I reach for my phone and silence it. I stayed up much too late trying to occupy my mind last night, only to finally fall asleep to an early episode of Friends.

I know you're not supposed to, but I have the horrible habit of scrolling through my phone when I first wake up.

There's a text from Will that came in at eleven-thirty, which I never saw.

Will: *How in the hell did you manage that?*

I read the text three more times, sure that I've missed something in the fog that I'm in.

I begin my text, only to retype it because it was all gibberish, since I'm not fully functional and awake yet.

Me: *What did I manage to do?*

I adjust my pillow and watch my phone. It's only six o'clock in the morning. Surely he's not sitting on the other end just waiting for me.

And what if he's not alone?

Those three little dots pop up and I sit up in my bed.

Will: *Good morning, sunshine. Surely you're not really up, are you? You're never out of bed this early.*

Me: *I'm still in bed. I saw your text from last night. What did I do?*

There's a bit of me that's hoping he'll call me because it would mean that he is alone. Instead, he texts again.

Will: *The note*

Me: *What note?*

Will: *The secret admirer note you left in my takeout box. The one with the hearts, and the I love yous*

I don't care who is in his bed, I push the contact and call him.

"Good morning," he says easily but sleepily.

"I didn't leave you a note," I say, now sitting straight up in my bed, pushing my unruly curls from my eyes.

"Sure you did."

"I think I would have known if I did," I say.

There's a moment of silence before Will says anything. "You didn't give me the note?"

"No."

"Then who did?" he asks.

"Why would I know that? Who sent me the bear and the flowers?" I ask.

"I don't know," he says and then lets out a breath. "Do you think someone is messing with us?"

"Obviously. And are you alone?" I finally ask, though I don't want the answer.

"Yes, why wouldn't I be?"

Is he clueless?

"I mean, isn't Brandy with you?"

"No. She's not here with me. She's in her own room."

"Why?" I just can't help myself.

Will lets out a little laugh. "Why would she be with me?"

"C'mon, isn't that what you want?"

"What I want is for her not to hate me. What I want is for her to talk to me if we're going to live together."

"Don't you want her back?"

"Mon, even if that happens, we have a lot of work to do to

mend our issues. A few good nights of conversation aren't going to fix what broke us up."

Seriously, he must be the most mature person I've ever known. I would have taken any conversation from an ex as a sign that we were back in love and supposed to move on. Will takes the time to consider what's happening.

"I need to get ready for work," I say.

"Me too. Do you have time for lunch?" he asks.

"Yeah."

He chuckles. "I'll pick you up and we'll walk down to the Cheesecake Factory."

"Yeah, okay."

"And, Mon, I love you," he says, and it settles me, just like it always does.

"Yeah, I love you too."

18

WILL

I stare down at the note that I took out of the takeout container as I pack up my sandwich. Usually I work at home on Fridays, but today is one of those days I have to be in the office.

And I know Monique and I made lunch plans, but sometimes she cancels. If I don't take my sandwich I ordered last night with me, I'll be starving if she doesn't make it to lunch. One thing about having so many women in my life, I've learned to just be prepared for anything.

I don't know what had made me look in the container last night and find the note. Any note would have been from Monique, and she hadn't been there.

I take a mental inventory of the staff that works on Thursdays. Does one of them know about this little game Monique and I are playing? When I didn't walk in with her, did someone take it upon themselves to have a little fun and leave the note?

The door to Brandy's bedroom opens, and she steps out in a pair of jeans and a polo shirt with her company's logo on it.

She smiles as she looks in my direction. I smile back.

"Good morning," she says.

"Good morning," I say.

"Packing up your lunch?"

"Sure am."

"Are you leaving?" she asks.

"Yeah, I have to be in the office today," I say.

Her lips twist, pucker, and then she smiles again. "Well, I hope you have a nice day."

"I will," I say, looking down at the note and then back up at her as she walks through the living room, gathers her purse, and heads out the door.

I shake my head. Brandy left me the note. We might not have been on speaking terms for months, but we dated long enough that I know when she's hiding something. And now, looking at the note objectively, I recognize the handwriting.

I pick up my phone and text Monique.

Me: *I figured it out*

Monique: *And?*

Me: *Brandy left me the note*

I wait for a response, surprised that I don't get one right away.

I finish packing my lunch and making my coffee, then I head out. It isn't until I'm in the elevator of my office building that Monique texts me back.

Monique: *How do you know it's from her?*

Me: *Is it from you?*

Monique: *I told you it wasn't*

Me: *It was just how she reacted to it*

Monique: *I can't go to lunch today*

The doors open and I step out on my floor, still studying my phone. That was an abrupt change to the conversation.

Me: *Okay. Call me later*

Monique: *Sure*

I start to text her that I love her, but I stop. I'm not feeling settled with her reaction to the secret admirer note. It's supposed to be exactly the end to her plan, right? Monique started this so that Brandy would pay attention to me. Now Brandy is leaving me notes, and Monique won't pay attention to me.

There's a heaviness in my chest when I think about it like that.

---

At lunch time, I eat my sandwich in my office, looking out over the city. It's cold and people on the street hurry from one building to another with their coats zipped up.

I take a bite of my sandwich and set it back on the napkin on my desk. For some reason it's just not satisfying today.

When my phone dings, I quickly pick it up, hoping that Monique has something to say that will brighten my day.

It's a text from Brandy, and I open the text with a feeling of dread.

Brandy: *How is your lunch?*

I pick up another napkin and wipe my mouth and my fingertips before replying.

Me: *It's okay*

Brandy: *Would you be interested in dinner? There's a new place just down the street from our place. I thought we could try it*

I study the text. *Dinner. Our place.* These are the kinds of texts I used to get. This is what I've been waiting for since we called it quits.

Just to make sure I haven't missed anything, I scroll through my texts and see that Monique hasn't texted me again all day. Maybe she's giving me space. Maybe she ran into her boss again and things are going well for her too.

Me: *That sounds nice. I'll meet you at home*

Brandy: *I can't wait.*

She adds three little hearts to her text.

I let out a long breath.

Brandy is talking to me and now leaving me secret admirer

notes that say she loves me, and yet, all I can think about is the fact that Monique is ghosting me today.

Maybe I should head over to her office and make sure she's okay. I mean, since the seventh grade she's never ghosted me.

I push my phone to the side of the desk as if to make it appear, to myself, unimportant.

Monique has a life and I need to not worry that she needs to communicate with me every moment of her day. But then again, I think, as I pull the phone near me, I'm not used to her not being in every single moment of my day.

I pull up her text thread and look down at it.

This borders on obsession, I consider as I wipe my mouth again with the napkin.

Me: *Everything okay?*

Like some puppy waiting for its owner, I sit and wait. And wait. And wait.

I guess I need to do more than text.

Gathering up my lunch items, I scroll to the app for the coffee shop down the street from Monique's office. I order two coffees and head out.

# 19

## MONIQUE

I have ten different reports on my desk that need my attention. One of my data processors took a leave of absence, and no one has picked up her workload.

This is what I've been expecting since Jay Cresswell took over as the new CEO. New bosses come with a ton of new work, and I guess I was the only one that saw that coming.

When I look up from the pile on my desk, Jay is standing in my doorway holding two cups of coffee from the coffeehouse down the street. One of the cups is the frozen coffee I always get.

He's grinning at me, and I have no doubt that I'm staring up at him with a look that can't be friendly.

"Do you have time for coffee?" he asks as he steps into my office and closes the door behind him with the help of his foot and his hip.

I lick my lips because they've gone dry. "Um, sure," I say as Jay walks to my desk and sets the coffees down.

He pulls a wad of napkins from his pocket and sets my drink on one, obviously aware of the condensation that it gives off.

"I think that's your drink, right?" he asks.

I nod. "How did you know that?"

"It's what your secret admirer delivered that one time."

I make an O with my mouth. Yes, in fact, my secret admirer had sent me one. I can't help but smile when I think of Will sending me things. I guess it did its job. Jay Cresswell paid attention.

Jay sits down in the chair on the other side of my desk, and then he scoots it closer so that he can lean over the top of my desk. It's a fairly intimate move.

"How are things going?" he asks.

I look over the top of my desk as I take a sip of my frozen coffee through the straw. I'm careful to not sip too hard. Brain freeze is not what I'm going for here.

"There's a lot going on right now," I say. "But we'll get there."

"It's a little overwhelming when someone new comes in, isn't it?"

I shrug. "It's expected."

Jay smiles and I realize just how white his teeth are. "I'll try not to overwhelm you too much."

He sits back in his chair and sips his coffee. He looks comfortable, and as if he's here to stay for a while.

"Have you ever been to Emilio's?" he asks.

I raise a brow. "No, Emilio's? Where is that?"

"Downtown. Not too far from here."

Jay sips his coffee again. "Would you be interested in going tonight for dinner?"

I blink up at him a few times. My stunned silence has caused him to grin at me.

"You want to take me to dinner?"

He leans in on my desk again, and that's when I notice just how perfectly manicured his fingers are and how expensive his watch is. This man is the whole gorgeous package.

"I do want to take you to dinner."

"But—"

He holds up a hand. "I know. I'm your boss. I realize this is probably not the best timing. I checked out the HR handbook, and there isn't anything that says we can't date. I mean, it does say that management needs to be alerted, but I *am* management."

I swallow hard. "You are that."

"So what do you say? Will you go out with me?"

I run my tongue over my lips because they've gone dry, but he watches me. This is what I wanted, right? This was where I wanted this to go.

Before I can answer, there is a tapping at the door.

Jay and I exchange looks before he gathers his cup of coffee, moves to the door, and opens it.

Standing on the other side of the door is Will with two coffees in his hands, and one is a frozen coffee, just like the one on my desk.

"Oh, hey," he says, shifting a look between me, Jay, the coffee on my desk, and the door which had been closed. "I didn't mean to interrupt."

Jay smiles. "No problem. I was just heading back to my office," he says and then turns his attention back to me. "So, dinner?"

I look at Will and then at Jay. "Yeah. I'll wait for you when we're done."

He nods and excuses himself from the office.

Will steps in and watches as Jay walks down the hall. "I interrupted something."

"Yeah, you did," I say, lifting the frozen coffee I already have on my desk.

Will looks at the frozen coffee he's holding. "I just wasted six bucks, didn't I?"

"Val likes those too," I say. "Why are you here? It's the middle of the day."

"Yeah," he says as he moves toward my desk. "I just wasn't getting a good vibe from you this morning and I was worried."

I narrow my eyes on him. "You were worried?"

"You don't usually ghost me."

I sit back and cross my arms. "I ghosted you?"

"It felt like it."

"I have never ghosted you. Ever," I say again. "If I'm not mistaken, you ghost me."

"When have I ever ghosted you?"

I snort out a laugh. "When you and Brandy are together, you ghost me. She doesn't like me, Will. The minute you two are back together full time, you'll ghost me."

"I will not."

"You can't say that. Wasn't our friendship part of what tore you apart?"

His lips purse because he knows I'm right. Sure, he never would confirm that because he doesn't ever want to hurt my feelings, but I know it's true.

"That won't happen," he promises, but I know he can't make that promise firmly.

I draw in a breath and study him. "I didn't mean to ghost you. I have a lot of work to do," I say, but deep down, I think I'm jealous and I'm only now acknowledging that is what's going through me.

Will deserves better than Brandy, and it's tearing me up a bit to know that my game is what got her talking to him again.

He hands me the frozen coffee. "See if Val wants it."

"Thanks for thinking of me and stopping by."

"I needed to make sure everything was okay." He looks toward the door and then back at me. "It seemed pretty cozy in here with you and the boss."

I pick up my drink and take a sip through the straw as I grin up at him. "He asked me out."

Will's brows rise. "Yeah, I heard. And that's allowed?"

I shrug. "He says he checked HR and we're good."

"Well, congrats. It looks like we're both getting what we want."

## 20

## WILL

As I walk up to my apartment, I'm still replaying the conversation with Monique in my head. She didn't even realize she was ghosting me. She's going out with her boss. She was short with me.

Why am I worried about this? Monique is her own person. She's dated plenty of men, and I've never worried about it before, but I can't help but think that dating her boss is a bad idea.

As I put my key in the door, it opens. Brandy is standing on the other side, smiling at me.

"I thought I heard you coming," she says.

"Yeah," is all I can think to say.

"Are you ready to go?"

I blink at her and study her. "Um, sure. I just need a few minutes."

"Sure," she says, stepping back and letting me through the door.

I hang my messenger bag on the hook, take my lunch box and coffee mug to the kitchen and set them on the counter, and then head to my bedroom to change.

I suppose it's out of habit, but I close my door. I just need a few moments.

Pulling my phone from my pocket, I click on my text thread with Monique.

Me: *Have a nice evening*

Monique: *I will*

Me: *Call me if you need me to come and rescue you*

Those three dots pop up, go away, pop up again.

Monique: *I don't need your heroics. I'll be fine*

Me: *Great. I wouldn't want to be interrupted tonight anyway*

Monique: *Perfect*

That is the end of our conversation. I don't like where our friendship has gone. We're both getting what we want, but I can't help but think that I'm losing my best friend at the same time.

---

Brandy must have been saving all of her conversations with me for this night. As we walk to the restaurant, she commands the conversation, and I'm not sure she's taken a breath.

"What do you think?" she asks.

I turn my head and look at her. "What?"

"What do you think? Red or yellow?"

I realize I haven't been listening to her at all. "Red?"

She lets out a little hum. "I don't know. Yellow is a more friendly color, don't you think? It'll be easier to paint over when we move."

"When we move?"

"Well, our lease is up in four months. I guess painting the bathroom now is silly, really."

Is that what she was talking about? Is she thinking we won't renew our lease? Is she moving out? Am I?

"Here it is," she says as we approach the restaurant. "I don't know why I can't remember the name of this place."

I look up at the sign. *Emilio's*, the marquee says.

I pull open the door, and Brandy walks through. She walks to the host stand and gives them her name for the reservation that she made.

The host walks us to our table and seats us with our menus.

I wait until Brandy takes off her coat and gloves, and I set them on the extra chair before I take off my coat and set them on the chair as well.

She's studying the menu before I sit down. "I've heard they have amazing steaks and lobster. Oh, and look at that martini on the drink menu."

I sit down and pick up my menu, but I'm distracted by Monique walking past us with her boss.

Of course she doesn't have on a coat, but he does. He didn't even bother to give it to her to cover her up in that dress she has on. Some gentleman.

Her boss' hand is low on her back. I grip the menu tighter and watch as they are seated in a corner booth, and now out of my sight.

"Should we share?" Brandy asks, and once again, I realize I'm not listening to her at all.

"Sure," I say, closing the menu.

"Will you order? You always order best."

I press my fingers to the bridge of my nose, and Brandy eases in on her elbows to lean in toward me.

"What's wrong with you? You're not listening to anything I'm saying tonight."

I purse my lips and point toward the corner where Monique disappeared with her date.

"Monique and her boss just walked through."

There's no masking the disappointment on Brandy's face when I say that.

"Handy," she says, picking up the menu again, looking at it, and then closing it again. "Why is she here?"

"I don't know."

"Really?"

"Really."

"It's interesting how wherever you are, she's there. Or if you're not there, she calls upon you to save her."

This is more like it, I think. This is how things were with Brandy before we broke things off.

Monique was right. Our fights usually stemmed from my relationship with her.

"So she's on a date with her boss? That's so tacky," Brandy says, craning her neck to get a better look, though I know she can't see anything.

"It's just dinner."

"Sure," she draws out the word before turning her attention back to me. "I'm sorry. I know she's your best friend and all."

I don't have anything I can say to that. She is my best friend, and I've spent many years defending that relationship.

The server takes our order, and Brandy and I sit in silence. I don't want things to be awkward between us, but they are, and all because of her feelings for Monique's friendship with me.

2 1

# MONIQUE

Jay has great taste. This restaurant is amazing. He ordered us a bottle of wine and our dinners. I don't usually go on dates with men that order my food for me, but I don't mind. There's something sexy about it.

We are seated next to one another in the booth, which is intimate, considering this is only our first date.

When the wine is delivered, Jay pours me a glass, and then one for himself.

I thank him, and then realize he has his glass raised as if in a toast, so I lift mine as well.

"To us," he says.

Why do I think that's so forward? I don't say anything in response. Instead, I tap my glass to his, and that's when I see the back of Brandy's head.

Jay turns his gaze to meet mine. "What's the matter?"

I ease back in my seat. "I just saw someone I know," I say.

"Did you want to go say hello?"

"No," I answer quickly.

He slowly nods at that, but then smiles at me.

"I've been very impressed with how well you've adapted to all the work I've been giving you. I promise it'll slow down," he says.

"Oh, I've been through that before. I know."

"I have a confession to make," he says, sitting with his arm on the back of the booth behind me. He leans in closer to me so that he can talk in my ear. "I'm your secret admirer."

I pull back from him and study him. "You're what?"

"I'm your secret admirer."

I blink hard. Is he kidding me with this? Will is my secret admirer.

No, Will didn't send the huge bouquet of roses or the enormous bear.

"You're my secret admirer?"

"Well, one of them," he laughs. "The bear and the flowers."

I nod in understanding. "That's very unexpected."

"I didn't mean to be so mysterious. I just thought it would be fun. I didn't know you had another secret admirer."

Looking at the table across the restaurant, at the back of Brandy's head, I shake my own. "I don't really another secret admirer," I say.

Jay's brows rise as he takes a sip of his wine and then sets the glass back down on the table. "You didn't send yourself those coffees and the bagel, did you?"

I let out a little giggle. "No, they were sent to me, but from my best friend."

His lips tighten, as if he's trying to hold in a laugh.

"Your best friend?"

"Yes. It was kind of a joke. I sent him some notes so his ex would see them," I say, lifting my wine glass and taking a sip of the wine, which is wonderful and expensive, and not something I could ever buy on my own.

"So why did he send them to you?"

I study him. He's the vision of perfection. Beautiful eyes, with only a hint of lines when he smiles. That square jaw and perfect hair.

His well-manicured fingers are wrapped around his wine-glass, and when he lifts it to his lips, his big, expensive watch jostles on his wrist.

I consider what he's asked me. I'm certainly not going to tell Jay that Will sent them so that he would notice me. I guess he'd noticed me on his own. Well, that's a dumb thought. Of course he noticed me. We ran right into one another with coffee splashing between us, and then I got knocked out right in front of him, too.

"I think he was just making me feel good because I was worked up over not having a date for Valentine's Day," I say.

"That's not for another month," he says.

"I know. It was just something I was focused on."

"Well, he sounds like a good friend."

I look again toward Brandy, who is almost out of sight because she's leaned so far over the table now.

"He's the best," I admit, taking another sip of my wine and turning my attention back to my dinner date.

Jay eases closer to me. "I have no doubt you'll have a date for Valentine's Day," he whispers intimately, and it causes me to draw in a deep breath.

Easing back from him, I study his face. I was not prepared for this.

I clear my throat. "So, tell me all about you."

---

Dinner was . . . interesting.

Jay is a great guy. I think I could spend a lot of time with him, but my mind wasn't focused on him—it was focused on the fact that Brandy and Will were only feet away from me.

Let's face it, I think I made a huge mistake.

I don't want them together, but I have no say in the matter. What is done, is done, and because of me, Brandy is now talking to him.

They live together. Now, I guess everything is just as it used to be, only this time, I can guarantee that Brandy isn't going to let me spend time with Will.

My heart is breaking, and in this moment, I should be ecstatic because I got to go on a date with a man I find irresistible. Jay is kind, and warm, and very attentive. He told me all about his life and how he came to work for the company. It was comfortable.

Now, laying in my bed, staring at the blank screen on my phone, I want to text Will. I don't want things to change if it means I don't have him in my life.

I'd rather we both be miserable and alone together than for him to be with Brandy.

It's so unfair, but I can't help it.

Just as I decide I'm going to text him to see how his evening was, knowing full well that my text won't be answered because Brandy is there, my screen lights up.

Will: *Are you awake?*

Me: *Yes*

Will: *Are you alone?*

I turn onto my stomach and rest my phone on the pillow. My hands are shaking now and I can't hold it without dropping it.

Me: *Yes, I'm alone*

A moment later, my phone rings and I roll back over and answer it.

"Hi," I say.

"Hi," Will says. "How was your date?"

"Good, though I was distracted knowing you were just at the other table."

He lets out a low hum. "Yeah, I was surprised when you guys walked through."

"How come you didn't say hi?" I ask, wondering why we're talking about this now but we ignored each other at the restaurant.

"Mon, you know that I—"

"I know," I say, not wanting to hear an excuse from him about how Brandy feels about me.

"Ya," he says and goes silent for a beat. "So, how was the date, really? He's a good guy? You like him?"

I roll to my side, tucking my phone under my head. "He is a nice guy. He's sweet and kind," I say. "He's also my secret admirer."

"I'm your secret admirer," he says seriously.

"The other one. He's the one that sent the flowers and bear."

"Ohhh," Will says, drawn out. "I'm happy for you, Mon."

I don't want to ask about his date with Brandy, but I feel as if I need to.

"How was your date?"

Again, he's silent for a moment. "Well," he sighs. "I don't think it was as good as your date."

I need to work to keep my voice even, because him saying that has me sitting up in bed and grinning.

"I'm sorry," I say, and I hope it conveys correctly, no matter how I mean it. "What happened?"

"It's not important. I just realize that maybe there was a reason that we broke up."

Even though I'm thrilled that it's not working out for them, I can't help but feel sorry for him.

"Do you want to come over?" I ask.

"I don't think that would help. But I'll see you next Thursday for dinner, right?"

I'm torn. The fact that he wants to do dinner without her is good, but he's miserable and I can't help him.

"Of course, I'll be at dinner."

"I'll see you then," he says as if that's the end of the call.

Before he can hang up, I say, "I love you."

He chuckles, "I love you, too, Mon."

## 22
## WILL

It's been a long weekend. Brandy has been flitting around the apartment, moving things out of her bedroom and into the shared space. I guess that dinner on Friday night was only awkward for me.

I suppose Brandy didn't realize that she'd ruined the entire night by her comments or her attitude toward Monique.

I should have said something. Heck, I should have said something years ago, and I never did. Well, when I did, we broke up.

She's been touching me as she passes me in the hallway, or while we're both in the kitchen. The crazy thing is, I don't feel a thing.

We haven't kissed, or moved our relationship back to what it was, but I think that's what she's thinking is going on.

Strange thing is, it was what I wanted, but not anymore. Stranger yet, it's not because of Brandy.

It's because of Monique.

When I was seventeen, I went through this. My best friend in the whole world was Monique Trafford. She was a cheerleader, a scholar, the lead in the musicals, a state-champion tennis player, and a fashionista. Of course, the fashionista part is still part of who Monique is.

But that year, our junior year in high school, Monique was all I thought about.

We'd established early on that we were friends and that was it. Chalk it up to hormones, I suppose, but she turned my head that year—mine and Chuck Thomas', whom she'd go on to date until senior year. It was enough to wake me from my pining for her, and our friendship endured.

For the first time in years, I'm feeling that again, and it's killing me.

I want to go back to when I didn't care who she dated. But what I realize, as I watch Brandy organize the knickknacks she'd taken out of the living room and was now replacing, I didn't care who she dated because I was the one in a long-term relationship. I was the one living with a woman and making plans that were never going to come to fruition.

Brandy winks at me as she moves about the living room. She's probably thinking it's her I'm thinking about, but it's Monique. And I realize that it's always Monique.

Text messages and phone calls. Coffee runs, lunch dates, and our usual dinner at the bar. Sleeping on her couch because I don't want to be alone, and not because I don't think she should be alone.

I'm allowed in her private spaces, in her refrigerator, in her closet. I'm the one she calls when she needs something. I don't care if she calls because she's lonely or she needs a safe ride home. I don't care that she uses me as her "boyfriend" when she needs one.

I certainly don't care that she kisses me.

A knot forms in my throat and I try to swallow it down.

She kissed me on New Year's, but that was my idea.

I kissed her when I picked her up from the bar, and that was her idea, but I let the kiss linger and I deepened it until my head was fuzzy.

"You're deep in thought," Brandy says as she moves toward me, this time sauntering right up next to me so that we're side by side.

"I am."

She bites down on her lip. "What are you thinking about?"

Nope, I can't tell her. I can't tell her that I need to talk to Monique, and that I've been thinking about her nonstop. I can't tell Brandy that the moment I saw Monique walk into the restaurant with her boss, I knew how I felt about her—really felt about her. I'm not out to break Brandy's heart, but I can't help that I might.

"I need to run out for a minute. Do you need anything?"

A crease forms between her brows. "I'm fine."

"I'll be back in just a bit," I say, stepping away from her and walking toward the front door to get my coat and keys.

"Will," she says, following me. "Are you okay?"

I nod. "I will be."

---

Pulling up to Monique's, I have no idea what I'm going to say to her. I don't really know what I'm feeling.

That's not true. I know what I'm feeling. I just need her to put me in my place.

My palms are sweaty, and my heart is racing.

This is the craziest thing ever. I've never been like this when it comes to Monique, but at this moment, those kisses are playing in my head, and knowing Brandy is at home moving her stuff back into place is killing me.

As I round the corner, the door opens, and Monique and her boss walk out. Again, she's in a tight little dress and she has to be freezing. Her boss has his arm around her, but didn't encourage her to wear a coat or even give her his.

Her hair is down and straight, which I know she hates to do because of the time it takes. As they walk, she laughs, and that silky mane sways, and then she rests her head on his shoulder.

Everything inside of me aches.

I may be wrong in thinking about Monique in the way that I am, but I certainly don't want her with anyone but me—even as friends.

But this isn't my call.

As her best friend, I need to be happy for her and encourage her.

Turning back, I walk to my car, open the door, and just sit inside. My breath carries on the frozen air, but I can't move.

I pull out my phone and text her.

Me: *Hey! Whatcha doing?*

I wait for a moment before my phone pings.

Monique: *Going out. I'll talk to you later*

Me: *Okay. Be careful. Text me when you get home*

To that, I get no reply.

Me: *I love you*

And again, I get no reply.

## 23
## MONIQUE

The stack of papers on my desk is triple the size it was last week. I feel like I'm drowning and as if I'm not doing my job right. I've been working solidly for the past three days, even staying at work for an extra two hours each night.

Of course, that works out because Jay takes me to dinner after.

"Did you fall behind, or are they tripling your workload?" Val asks as she walks into my office with yet another folder to hand me.

"This company isn't making any more money than before, but the bookkeeping is triple," I say.

"Every department head's desk looks like this. Seriously, Mon, can't you say something to him?"

I narrow my gaze on her. "To who?"

She laughs. "Your new boyfriend."

My entire body tenses at that.

"My new boyfriend?" My voice cracks as I say it.

Val leans in over my desk. "Mon, everyone knows you're seeing the boss. Can't that work to your advantage?"

"I didn't tell anyone I'm seeing him."

"You don't have to. Is it not public knowledge?" she whispers.

"No."

She eases back. "Got it. No more gossip about the boss."

"Val!"

"I'm kidding. I'm happy for you. I mean, if you're happy and all. By the look of your desk, I can't see where you would be happy."

"I am happy."

"Good. And what about the guy you were kissing at the bar?"

My shoulders fall. "I told you, he's just my friend."

"Yeah, you said that. But I still saw the kiss," she says and shrugs before turning and walking out of my office.

I lean back in my chair.

I felt that kiss. I *still* feel that kiss.

Picking up my phone, I open my texts.

I never did text Will back the other night. By the time I'd gotten home, I'd just forgotten. And the past two days have been nothing but work. I haven't had any time to think about anything else.

Will has been the one person since the seventh grade who could cheer me up when I'm down, or in this case, confused and overwhelmed.

Me: *Hey!*

Will: *Hey!*

I contemplate what I'm going to say next. I can't let him know that the past few days I've been miserable. I mean, I'm dating the boss. This is what I wanted. This is what he wanted for me.

Me: *We're still on for dinner tomorrow?*

Will: *Of course. Do you want to bring your boss?*

Just as I begin to type my answer rejecting that idea, another text from Will comes through.

Will: *Brandy is coming*

All I can do is stare down at my phone. I set it on the top of my desk because my hands are shaking. I feel sick.

I want to be mad and tell him that's unacceptable. Thursday nights are our nights.

I want to cry because I've lost him. Brandy inviting herself to our dinner night makes it about them—not us.

Okay, that's not fair. This is what Will wanted, and now it's what he's got. I suppose I should be thankful that Brandy wants to come, but I'm not. That's my time with my dearest friend.

I want to talk about what's going on between me and Jay. I'm not enjoying this new relationship with my boss like I thought I would be. I'm overworked. I'm confused. I miss Will.

Me: *I'll see if he's available. Are you sure?*

Will: *Sure. I'll see you tomorrow, Mon*

And that ends our conversation. No *I love you.* No extra banter.

"You look deep in thought," Jay says from my doorway as he walks into my office and closes the door behind him.

I nod. "I guess I was." I turn my phone over and study him.

His sleeves are rolled up, and I realize I've never seen him do that. There are dark circles under his eyes, and he's not cleanly shaven.

"Is everything okay?" I ask as he walks around my desk, takes my hand, and guides me to my feet.

Wrapping his arms around me, Jay pulls me in close to him, nuzzling his face into my neck.

Okay, this is new. He's been flirty when we're at the office, but he's never been affectionate like this.

He holds me in place for a few breaths and then eases back so that our foreheads are pressed together.

His eyes search mine. I don't know what answers he's looking for, but there is something wrong.

"Jay . . ."

I say his name a moment before he presses his lips to mine.

There's heat in the kiss, but I'm afraid it's not lit by passion. There's something more here. Angst. Pressure. Resentment.

His hand comes to the nape of my neck and anchors me there. But just as swiftly as he started the kiss, he ends it.

We're both panting, because it sucked the air right out of our lungs.

"I have to let you go," he says.

I blink hard and take a staggering step back, but his hands linger on my waist.

"What?"

"I have to let you go," he says again.

Studying him, I take another step from him to distance us now.

"Let me go?"

Jay runs his hand down his face, and now he looks more tired than he had when he walked in. His gaze scans over my desk before he looks back at me.

"You're not keeping up, and—"

"You mean my work?" I blurt out the words, trying to understand what he's saying. "I'm not keeping up?" My hands fly up as if they're not even attached to me. "I'm not keeping up?"

Jay points to my desk. "Look at all the work you're not—"

"Not what?" I step to him. "I'm working my butt off here, and you know it. I'm here early—with you. I'm here late—with you. The work just keeps coming. How am I supposed to catch up when you're burying me with it?"

"The higher ups just think—"

"Higher ups? You're the freaking CEO. There is no higher up."

With that interruption, he licks his lips. "They're replacing me too," he says, and that has my shoulders dropping.

"Because you're overworking your team?" I ask, and it's filled with a hurtful tone, which comes from my heart.

There is a tapping at my door before Val eases it open. I'm glad we're separated. Gossip was one thing, someone walking in on us while we were kissing, that would have been something bad.

"Mr. Cresswell, there is a woman here to see you," she says as she steps back, and I see a blonde woman with an empty box in one hand and a toddler on her hip.

Jay nods and walks toward the door. "We're supposed to be out of the building by five," he says before he walks through my door and closes it behind him.

I can't breathe. Did I really just get fired by my boyfriend?

I'm not going to stand for this. I've worked here for two years. I'm the head of the department. This place ran just fine before they brought in the sexy new CEO, and I'm not going to lose my job over it.

Sucking in a breath, I walk to the door, and pull it open. Val is just on the other side, and her eyes are wide. I must have startled her.

There's no time to chat, even though she's calling after me. I'm on a mission. A mission to tell Jay Cresswell just what I think of his CEO skills.

When I make it to his office, the door is open only the slightest bit, and I push it open.

The blonde woman who was standing in the hallway just a few minutes ago is loading things from Jay's desk into the box she was carrying, and he's holding the toddler that had been on her hip.

They all look up at me as I burst through, and Jay winces.

"Monique," he says my name softly, almost apologetically.

The woman moves in next to him, as if she's being protected by him, or is protecting him.

"This is my wife and our son."

## 24

# WILL

The bar is quieter than normal. There is a storm brewing outside, and snow swirls under the glow of the streetlights. I don't mind winter and snow, but the darkness at five o'clock, that I could do without.

I hoped that Monique would arrive before Brandy. I haven't talked to her in days. But when the door opens, Brandy hurries in.

She stomps the snow from her boots and brushes the flakes from her coat.

"Whew," she says as she walked toward the table. "It's really coming down. You already got your drink?"

I look at the beer in front of me. Had she expected me to wait for her?

I watch her and then realize I haven't stood to greet her.

Hopping off of my stool, I move to her, taking her coat as she begins to shrug out of it.

"Thank you," she says, and I take her coat and hang it over the back of her chair. I keep my eyes on the door, waiting for Monique to walk through on the arm of her boss, but she doesn't.

Brandy sits down, rubbing her arms with her hands. "Did you order already?"

"Not yet," I say as I take my seat next to her.

"I'm thinking a salad this week. I can't keep doing fried food," she laughs.

Brandy rests her hand atop mine, and I look at it as if I'm trying to figure out what she's doing. Then I lift my eyes to meet hers.

"You're distracted," she says. "Is everything okay?"

"I have a lot on my mind, I guess," I say, moving my hand out from under hers and picking up a menu. I don't even see anything on the menu, it's all a blur, but it's occupying my mind until the server comes to the table.

I check my phone, but there is no message or missed call from Monique, so I sit silently while Brandy talks about her day.

"I'm going to run to the restroom," Brandy says, hopping off of her stool. She's been talking since she walked in the door, but I haven't heard a word she said. "If the server comes back, get me a water, please."

I nod as she hurries away. That's when I notice the paper on the ground next to her chair.

I move from my seat to pick it up, assuming she's dropped her napkin. It's not a napkin.

Opening the folded paper, I look down at it.

Monique,
I know you're the one sending Will the secret admirer notes. It's time you move on. We're back together now.
Brandy

I swallow hard as I read the note over and over again. When the server comes by and asks if we need anything, I ask for the check for my beer.

My stomach clenches looking at the note again. So, Brandy was just going to give this to Monique? As if this is acceptable?

I pinch the bridge of my nose because there is a throbbing behind my eyes now.

"Monique and her boss still aren't here?" Brandy's voice has me lifting my head. "Seriously, how much longer are we supposed to wait for them? This is very inconsiderate," she says as the server drops off the bill for our drinks.

Brandy's eyes narrow on the check. "Are we leaving?"

I take in the sight of her standing in front of me. I'm confused to how oblivious I've been to her mean spirit. I mean, I knew she didn't like Monique because we were friends, but this . . .

My relationship with Monique is the only thing I've had my entire life. It's the thing I cherish more than anything else. That relationship has always been something that has caused a rift between Brandy and me. I should have talked to Monique when I went to her place and saw her with her boss. I should have told her what I was feeling, and we could have sorted it out. I won't make that mistake again.

"I'm ready to go," I say as I stand from my seat.

A smile forms on Brandy's lips. "We haven't eaten dinner yet. What are we going to do?"

I pull my wallet from my pocket and set the money on the table. Then I take the note that I found on the floor and hand it to Brandy.

She looks down at it as if she's never seen it before. But when she opens it, her face loses color.

"Will . . ."

"It's time for me to go."

"I can explain this," she says.

"You don't have to. You have no idea how much clarity this gives me."

"Monique wrote you those secret admirer notes," she blurts as I pull on my coat. "Well, not all of them. I wrote one. But we belong together. She has no right to you."

That has me stopping to look at her, my arm only halfway into my coat.

"No right to me?"

Brandy takes a step toward me, but my expression must stop her from advancing any further.

"Will, what I mean is—"

"I don't need to hear any more. Seriously, I should be thanking you," I say, shrugging my coat on fully and zipping it up. "I know she wrote the notes. It was to get your attention. It worked. You remembered we lived in the same house."

"Oh, Will—"

"I did the same for her."

"You wrote her secret admirer notes?"

Now I laugh. "I did. Well, I sent her secret admirer gifts."

Brandy crosses her arms. "Why would you do that if you were trying to get us back together?"

"To get her boss to notice her. This has all been a stupid game. Now she has him, and I realize something."

Her lips are trembling. "What?"

"I thought I wanted you. I was sure of it. I knew that if you'd just give me one more chance, it would work this time. But now I know it never will."

"Why? We can make this work," she pleads, and I now find that humorous. She's the one that broke it off. Now she wants me? Just because she thinks that Monique wants me?

I shake my head. "No, we can't make it work. Monique is always going to be in my life. That's a staple, and you can't make her go away. And we're not back together," I say.

Brandy's lips purse. "But we're working on it. And I just don't think it's appropriate for you to have her around when you're in a relationship."

I shake my head. "She's my dearest friend, and she was helping me out. And I was helping her out. Only now I realize I made a huge mistake. I put her in the path for someone else to love her, when all along it should have been me."

The color is back in Brandy's cheeks. "You love her?"

I nod. "I do. I've never faced it, but I do. I've loved her since the seventh grade. But if I couldn't have her, the next best thing was to be her best friend."

Brandy's eyes soften, her shoulders drop, and she sits back down on her stool. "You should go to her and tell her all of that."

I can't help but stand there and stare at her. Had she really said that?

"I'm serious, Will. There isn't anyone in this world that has been around the two of you that doesn't know there's a connection between you and Monique. And I know it better than anyone," she says.

"Really?"

She nods. "She's good for you—to you. Go. Go tell her all of this and maybe she won't chase her boss. She makes you happy. You should be happy."

I move to her and take her hand, easing her from her stool, and wrap her in a tight hug. "Thank you."

"Go, before I come to my senses," she says, her voice wet from tears that are welling in her eyes.

I kiss her on the cheek and nearly race out of the bar. I don't know why Monique didn't show up tonight, and sure, she's probably with her boss, but I can't wait to tell her how I feel. I've waited too long.

## 25
# MONIQUE

I suppose I should have seen this all coming. I'm not relationship material.

It would be nice to say that nothing like this has ever happened to me, but that would be a lie. I've started relationships with two other men who forgot to mention that they had a wife and kids. Yeah, it's like the Monique curse.

My entire office sits in a box on my kitchen table. Everything but that stupid big bear, which I left sitting in my chair.

I have to start over.

Sinking back down into my couch, the comforter from my bed wrapped around me, I pull it up over my head. Never, ever again am I going to date someone from work.

And that has me pulling my knees up to my chest.

We had the perfect meet cute, too.

I wrap the comforter around me tighter, only to nearly fall to the floor when I bolt straight up when someone knocks on my door.

This is a secure building, so when someone just knocks, it freaks me out. And the only people that can be knocking are my neighbors. Well, I'm not answering. No one needs to know I'm here.

"Mon. Mon, are you in there? Open the door."

I rub the back of my hand over my eyes and sit up.

It's Will. Okay, well, he's the only person I'd ever trust with a key, but he's never used it. He's not that kind of guy. So what is he doing knocking on my door? He's never just walked into the building, even though I gave him the key and told him he could come up any time.

"Mon, I'll come in if you don't answer. Honey, are you okay?"

He knows something. His voice has that quiver when he's worried about something.

Hauling myself off the couch, the comforter still wrapped around me, I start for the door. When I pull it open, his keys dangle from it. He was serious, I guess.

"You're okay?" he says, stepping toward me.

"Do I look okay?"

"No. You don't."

I turn and walk back into my condo as he pulls his keys from the door. When he closes the door behind him, I turn back to him.

"You should be with your girlfriend. Why are you here? This will just piss her off."

There's a humored look in his eyes, and I don't understand that at all. There is nothing humorous going on here.

Will moves to me. He stands right in front of me and smiles down at me.

"I don't have a girlfriend," he says.

I'm so confused by this. "Will, I'm not in the mood."

I turn to walk back toward the couch, but he reaches for me, comforter and all.

"Mon, listen to me. I don't have a girlfriend."

I study him. He's grinning.

If he's telling me he doesn't have a girlfriend, he shouldn't be grinning.

"You and Brandy are—"

"Nothing," he says, inching in even closer.

His hand moves to my face, and he tucks a wayward curl behind my ear.

"Why are you home, alone, wrapped up in your comforter? You look as if you've been crying."

When he says this, his eyes soften with concern.

"Why are you here, Will?"

The corner of his mouth twitches. "To see you. You didn't show up tonight."

I let out a groan and turn from him. "Seriously, I'm not in the mood."

"Why are you home alone?"

"Will . . ." I collapse on the couch.

His eyes move to the box on my table, and the line between his brows deepens.

"Mon, what's going on?"

"What do you think?" I snap out the words.

"Why didn't you show up with your boss?"

Now he sounds worried, and this is more like it. What the hell was with the ginning and coming into the building? I seriously think he's lost his mind.

And wait! Did he say he *didn't* have a girlfriend?

"Why aren't you with Brandy at the bar?" I ask.

His grin is back, and he sits down next to me on the couch.

"That's not going to work out," he says.

"No kidding. But if it's what you want, then I want that for you."

He nods, considering what I've said. "She's not the right person for me," he says, reaching for my hand.

Will twines our fingers together. With his eyes on our hands, he shakes his head.

"I can't have both of you in my life."

I let out a groan. "That's her problem. You're my best friend, and I'm not just going to drop out of your life so that she—"

"I don't want her," he says.

I turn to face him, my hand still clasped in his.

"What?"

"Where's your boss?" he asks.

"Why does that matter?"

"Just tell me why you're here wrapped up in your bedding—alone."

I bat away tears that are stinging my eyes. "I don't know where he is. I assume he's home."

Will nods. "Why do you have a box on your table full of things from your office?"

Now I pull from him and stand, dropping the comforter. "I got fired. Okay? I got fired."

"Mon . . ."

I hold up my hand. "I was wrong about him, okay? Does that make you happy? I was wrong."

Will stands. "Why would that make me happy?"

"Because, well, I don't know. You warned me."

"I warned you about dating your boss. I wasn't warning you against anyone in particular."

"Well, maybe you should have."

He moves to me and gathers me into his arms. "Tell me what happened."

I rest my head on his chest. "First of all, he fired me for not doing my work."

"That's wrong."

"Right?" I wipe my nose with the back of my hand. "And then his wife and his kid show up to help him pack his office because they fired him too."

Will eases back from me. "Wife and kid?"

"No surprise, right? Monique Trafford again picks a winner. Now she's out of a job. She's single. She's disgusted with herself."

Will wraps his arms around me. "You're selling yourself short. You didn't make any mistake in this."

I look up into his eyes, which search my face. "Why are you single?"

The corner of his mouth turns up. "Because Brandy isn't the woman I want to be with. She never was."

I narrow my gaze on him. "I don't understand."

Will draws in a deep breath. "Mon, you're the woman I want to be with. You always have been."

26

WILL

Monique hasn't blinked in what feels like eternity. She's just staring at me.

This was the make or break moment. This was me opening up and accepting defeat if that's what's coming at me.

"Do you have anything to say?" I finally ask, because the silence is killing me.

She blinks now and her brows draw together.

"I don't understand what you're saying," she says.

"You're the smartest woman I know. I'm pretty sure you understand."

Monique pushes back from me. Turning, she walks toward the window which looks out to the city.

After a few silent moments, she turns back to look at me. Her eyes have lightened, and I wonder if she's finally figured it out.

"Me?" she says, and I smile.

"You."

"Will, you've always had me."

I nod. "But I want more, Mon. I want you."

Monique pulls her bottom lip through her teeth. "We're friends," she says.

Moving toward her, I step over the comforter and come to stand right in front of her. Everything inside of me wants to pull her to me, to kiss her, to hear her say she loves me as much as I love her. But I need to go slow.

"We're the best of friends," I say. "But, Mon, there has never been a day where I haven't loved you."

She licks her lips. "We say I love you to each other all the time."

I can't help but chuckle. "I think I usually say I love you, to which you say, 'Yeah, I love you too.'"

Her eyes go wide, and she cringes. "That sounds horrible."

"It's exactly what you would tell a friend," I say.

Monique swallows hard. "You're always here for me."

"I'll always be here for you. You can't get rid of me."

"I'd never want that."

I take another step so that we are now toe to toe. "Mon, I love you."

She takes a moment, just studying me. "As in actually love me?"

I chuckle. "As in actually love you."

"Will," she says my name on a breath as she places her hands on my chest, and I put my hands on her hips.

"Mon, it's always been you."

"You loved Brandy."

"I thought I did. I thought I needed to love someone other than you. But our breakup was proof that my love for you was always evident."

Monique lifts her hands to cup my face. Her dark eyes lock on mine.

"We've kissed," she says as if she's only now realizing how those kisses felt.

"We have," I confirm.

She lets out a little laugh. "They weren't," she sucks in a breath, "little kisses."

I lift my hand up into her hair. "No, they weren't."

Again, she licks her lips as she eyes mine. "Maybe we should have been kissing since we were twelve."

I can't help but smile at that. "We don't have to go any longer not kissing," I say, and her eyes lift to mine.

"Will, we can't do this," she says. "Our friendship."

I feel that sting in my chest, but I pull her in closer to me and her hands move from my face and her arms wrap around my neck.

"Our friendship only makes this better, Mon. I love you."

She studies my face, just as she had my mouth. "Will you kiss me again?"

I draw in a breath, watching her eyes, and as I ease in, her eyes close and her lips part. She's fighting me on this, but she wants this too. I love her and there is no reason to think that she doesn't love me too. She just needs to realize it in her own time, and I'll give her that time.

When my mouth comes to hers, Monique's entire body sways against mine, as if she's drunk and unable to stand. But when her mouth moves against mine, I know she's all in.

Her hand comes to the nape of my neck, and the kiss deepens. I hear the hum come from her throat, and I'm all but holding her up as we both drown in this moment.

When she needs breath, Monique eases back and her eyes flutter open to look up at me.

"I love you, Will. I have always loved you."

I'm sure the grin on my face is wide. I can feel it lift my cheeks. Monique Trafford loves me, and I know she doesn't just mean she loves me, her friend. Monique Trafford is in love with me, and I'm in love with her.

# EPILOGUE

## MONIQUE

**Valentines Day**

My goal had been to have a special someone by Valentine's Day. I had no idea I already had that someone in my life.

As the sun flows through my bedroom window, I stretch, and then pull Will's pillow to me. He left early this morning, kissing me softly before he headed to work.

He moved in the very day he told me he loved me, and I don't ever want him to leave.

Now I live with that regret of not having been his girlfriend since I was twelve. He says it just wasn't the right time until now. Since he's the smartest man I know, I think he's right.

My phone chimes on my nightstand, and I pick it up. It's Val.

*I brought donuts. I saved you three of them.*

I laugh. After Jay was fired, the new management called me back in to take back over my job. The feel in the office is much different, and the bonus is I don't start work until nine-thirty. The added bonus is that the new boss is a woman I worked with years ago.

And I wake up with Will every morning.

I push off the covers and roll out of bed. I walk to the bathroom and turn on the light to see the note Will wrote on the mirror with an erasable marker.

*Happy Valentine's Day! I love you!*
*Love, Your Secret Admirer*

The message has me grinning and grabbing my phone to take a picture of the message, careful not to get a glimpse of myself in the mirror.

———

I step into the elevator, coffee in hand and a coat on. Yes, some things just make sense now that I'm in a good relationship.

I watch the numbers climb as the elevator rises, and I'm still smiling, thinking about the note Will left for me on the mirror.

When the elevator door opens, Val is standing there waiting for me, donut in hand.

"Good morning," she says, handing me the donut on a small plate.

"Thank you," I say, curious as to why she's so adamant that I get a donut this morning.

"Carley was in here earlier and said she was going to give us all a half day off," Val says, mentioning our new boss.

"Why would she do that?" I ask as we walk toward my office.

"She says we all have better things to do on Valentine's Day."

As I place my hand on the knob to the door of my office, I look at Val who is standing beside me with an enormous smile. It's also when I notice that others are standing in their cubicles, looking over the walls at me.

I have to assume they've all eaten too many donuts and are on some kind of sugar high.

I turn the knob and push open the door to my office, and the scent of roses fills my nose first. Then I notice the petals on the floor that lead from the door to my desk, where there is a small bouquet sitting.

A smile tugs at my cheeks. I step inside and walk to my desk, where there is another note written in Will's handwriting.

*What do you say to spending every Valentine's Day from here on as my wife? Yes or No? (Please don't say no.)*
*Love, Your Secret Admirer*

The paper in my hand begins to shake. When I look up to ask Val what's going on, that's when I notice my parents standing in the doorway. My mother blows me a kiss as she walks into my office, my father right behind her.

Behind them are Will's mothers, and they, too, are grinning wide.

I lift my fingers to my lips and my eyes sting with tears.

Following his mothers in, Will walks toward my desk, and now I can see Val and everyone else in the office, including my boss, crowding at the door.

Will takes my hand and pulls me to him. The note still shakes in my hand.

"Looks like the cat is out of the bag," he teases, nodding toward the letter. "It's no longer a secret that I'm your biggest admirer."

"Will," I say his name in a whisper.

"So? What do you say?"

I look back down at the note that he'd left on my desk.

I step away from him, pull a red pen from the cup on my desk, and circle my answer.

When I hand it back to him, Will never even looks down. His eyes are filled with tears, and I notice that his mother Sheila has pulled his mother Anna into her arms, and they are both crying.

"I love you, Mon," Will says softly.

"I love you, too."

His smile widens. I'm direct with saying the words now.

From his shirt pocket, he pulls out a ring and slips it on my finger.

I look down at the solitaire that he'd placed on my finger, and then back up at him.

"You circled yes," he says, and I nod.

"I would never say no to my secret admirer."

"I don't think I ever kept my feelings about you much of a secret," he says, and his mom Sheila makes some kind of noise in agreement.

I ease into Will's arms as I giggle at that. "I just never paid much attention," I say.

"I think we're on the same page now."

"We most certainly are."

Will eases back and cups my face in his hands. "I promise you happily ever after, Mon. I swear it."

# RATE AND REVIEW

We hope you enjoyed *Secret Admirer Pact* by Bernadette Marie. If you did, we would ask that you please rate and review this title. Every review helps our authors.

Rate and Review: Secret Admirer Pact

# MEET THE AUTHOR

Bestselling Author Bernadette Marie writes contemporary romances and believes in Happily Ever After. The married mother of five believes in love at first sight, quick love, and second chances. An avid martial artist, Bernadette Marie is a certified instructor and holds a third degree black belt in Tang Soo Do. She loves Tai Chi, traveling to Disney parks, and having lunch with friends. When not writing, or running her own publishing house, Bernadette is probably immersed in a Rom Com, from which she will often quote one-liners.

# OTHER TITLES FROM

## 5 PRINCE PUBLISHING

Visit 5 Prince Publishing
Christmas Cove *Sarah Dressler*
Composing Laney *S.E. Reichert*
Firewall *Jessica Mehring*
Vampires of Atlantis *Courtney Davis*
Liz's Road Trip *Bernadette Marie*
Back to the 80s *S.E. Reichert & Kerrie Flanagan*
Granting Katelyn *S.E. Reichert*
Ghosts of Alda *Russell Archey*
The Serpent and the Firefly *Courtney Davis*
Raising Elle *S.E. Reichert*
Rom Com Movie Club No.3 *Bernadette Marie*
Rom Com Movie Club No.2 *Bernadette Marie*
Rom Com Movie Club No.1 *Bernadette Marie*
A Crossbow Christmas *Ann Swann*
Hot For Teacher *Felicia Carparelli*
The Happily Ever After Bookstore *Bernadette Marie*
Perfect Mrs Claus *Barbara Matteson*
Princess of Prias *Courtney Davis*